ISBN: 978-0-6487706-2-6

THE BEAST

JUDE PERERA

Illustrations by
VASANA PERERA

I dedicate this book to my loving wife, Vasana, my two beautiful boys, Viyan and Vivain, and to my beloved parents – I am what I am today, because of their love and affection.

CHAPTERS

ON THE TREEHOUSE

CHAPTER 1

THE WATCH

The mist was closing in fast and it was deadly cold. All members of the small group shivered violently, a mixture of cold and dread inspiring the shakes. The bewitching hour had already passed, and the Yakush had not made an appearance yet. Dylan was nodding off, Ash was super alert with the camcorder in one hand and the telescope in the other, Rose was happily humming a Tamil song tunelessly, and Menaka was missing her warm blankets and the heater at home. Dylan was exhausted after spending the last two hours gazing at Menaka and wishing that he could express his love telepathically.

He had spent more than a year trying to do the same when she lived over the fence. Then, when he was ready to lay every bit of his courage and dignity on the line, they had moved house. He had put it aside again, the distance eating in to his sudden swell of bravery.

Menaka and her mother had moved to a new house a few kilometres away. He adored everything about her; her super slim figure, olive complexion, shoulder length hair, dark eyes and that sweet dimpled smile that lit up her space and infected everyone else who happened to be in it. He even adored the rare butterfly-shaped birthmark on her right wrist. But now she had a huge crush on her piano teacher. Dylan had had every opportunity; their families had become good friends, he had convenience and access, but hadn't made a move. He feared losing his friendship with her. Dylan's sigh broke through louder than expected.

"You'll never ask her, you wuss, perhaps you might get your guts when she is an old grandmother with great grand children," Ash, short for Ashwin had rubbed it in one day at the playground. Dylan had punched him with a degree of lighthearted violence. He hated the truth. They were both seventeen and went to the same school – Trinity Catholic Boys College. He was sure that being in a boys' school had blunted his skill set and confidence around chicks, compounded by an unhealthy increase in curiosity for the damn creatures. He didn't want to blame it on his natural shyness, it was impossible to change that, but he was painfully aware of his thin and tall geeky looking frame, and his absolute lack of will to change it through hard work.

"You know I would have asked her the next day, what's the big deal, she could say yes or no, right?" Ash was brutally casual.

Dylan was jealous as hell of Ash's confidence; Ashwin was a freak of nature. He was a born charmer, and girls just buzzed around him. He had left a colourful trail of broken hearts with some of the prettiest girls in town – Dylan could only dream of some of them. Perhaps they even loved the stupid shock of well-manicured hair that he had generated just above his forehead. Dylan didn't want to think it was his nice tan or his athletic body built over years of playing sports; surely chicks weren't that stupid. Ash loved his soccer. And he was good in his grades. Dylan had gone nuts try-ing to work him out ever since they had become good friends. He wanted to learn the tricks.

"I respect them, I don't worship them like you do, you dork," Ash went on while casually executing a difficult backwards stretch. "Just buy her a box of those heart shaped Kandos chocolates for her sixteenth, and let's check out the reaction."

Ash had provided the strategy for Menaka's sixteenth birthday with a yawn.

"But what if she throws it in my face?" Dylan had brought forward his natural born worrier spirit.

"Well then I could eat it," Ash had laughed, ducking Dylan's anticipated blow.

They had bought the gift and Dylan had promptly switched it with a standard chocolate box at the last minute. She had sizzled that day in an embroidered organza dress; Dylan had approached her for the kiss on wobbly feet. She had turned her head just as he aligned his cheek with hers. Lips had met, and he suffered a near nervous breakdown. He had apologised, but words failed. She had turned away, a crushing blush blossoming on her face, and Ash had made matters worse.

"You know what? This guy bought a nice box of those heart-shaped chocolates, and swapped it for the one you got."

Dylan just wanted to breathe long enough to murder him.

"No way! I love that type. Shame, hope you haven't finished all of them Ash?" Menaka had said, making a sad face at Dylan.

"It's all done and digested," Ash said with a concocted burp. Dylan hated him for finishing the box.

He now looked at her with anguish, so close yet so far.

They were in the tree house on Ashwin's tea estate – which was right next to Horton Plains – built in the airy branches of a Willard mango tree. They could sense the mountains lording over them in the clouds. Pidurutalagala, the highest peak in the land, was among these giants. The plains spread next to them, a vast milky white ocean where forest and Sambar stood out like ghosts. The forest hid deadly predators like the leopard and the sloth bear. Sambar, a kind of deer, had come out in their dozens under the protective gaze of the dusk and mist.

They were on a mission; one million rupees lay at stake. The local Geographic Society had put it on offer for any solid evidence or footage of the Yakush. Was it fact or myth? This beast living deep in the forest had created quite a stir in their quiet city.

Yaku, devil in Sinhalese, had inspired the villagers to name it the Yakush. Villagers on the Horton Plains swore that their cattle and livestock were destroyed by it. They said that leopards were known to kill by a single throt-tle to the neck. But these creatures were killed by a vicious assault on their skulls, long teeth piercing the bone, and long claws tunneling deep in to the flesh with ease. Victims included the sambar that roamed the plains and the domestic cattle. They claimed that it attacked in thick mist or under the cover of darkness. There were suspicions that it was equally at home atop the trees and may launch aerial assaults on its terrified victims.

Some villagers had given chilling eyewitness accounts – bloodshot glow-ing eyes, velvety tawny skin, upright and super tall with the hind legs of a large cat. But it was its mournful and blood-curdling shriek that tormented them the most. Some children swore that they were attacked near Bakers Falls when they went for a dip in the icy cold waters. One had gone into shock and the Catholic priest had to bless him with holy water, which had healed him. There had been scratches on one of them, which catapulted him to instant fame, and he had granted himself a lifetime license for the bragging rights.

"Remember that guy with the allergy from the fake suit?" Rose broke the boredom with a loud laugh, blowing the wisp of hair that splashed itself permanently across her face.

They all caught the infectious dose of humour. A teenage boy in the village had dressed himself up as a Bigfoot type monster with his friends and had sent a photo to the competition. It was rumoured that the panel of experts had thrown it in the bin after one look, and the guy caught a skin rash from the fake fur. Rose yawned.

They all loved Rose, the dark, short Tamil girl with the waist-length hair and red pottu on her forehead who could never stop smiling. Her hair was carefully preserved due to a vow her parents had made at the local Hanuman Hindu Kovil for her good health. They didn't even know her surname, or if she had one, it didn't matter. She went to the local Tamil school. Her mother Meena had worked in Ashwin's father's estate at one time, and they had played together as children. Ash had introduced her to Dylan and Menaka, and they had found her impossible to resist. She was fifteen and had always suspected that her parents had named her after their favourite Tamil screen siren, Rose Balan, now an older star playing grandmotherly roles.

They had just finished a sweet supper of mangoes plucked straight off the branches that reached out in to the tree house. This was not long after gorging themselves with the sweet meats that Rose's mother had prepared for the late October Deepavali festival, also known as the festival of lights. An old goat bleated piteously at the foot of the tree, the one with one horn long and the other short. It was their bait to trap the Yakush. Apparently it enjoyed expensive taste and preferred the more expensive goat meat. Rose had borrowed it from Muruga uncle from her village. Menaka had insisted on its age, since she did not want its immediate kids and grandkids, if any, to miss it too much if their ruse worked.

"It's just a goat you idiot," Rose had laughed.

"I don't care," Menaka had come back with unusual venom.

"Ok… ok we'll select the oldest and the wisest," Rose laughed again, backing off though.

Menaka made a face.

"Hey by the way Prof, I have a question." Rose was on a roll.

"Yeaaah?" Dylan yawned. They called him Prof because he knew everything, or sometimes made it out as if he did. He loved the title.

"When are you and Menaka going to become a couple?" Rose came out in a single breath and hooted with laughter.

Dylan blushed, his light brown complexion doing its best to dress down the embarrassment, although he was half happy that she had asked. He looked straight at Menaka from behind the cover of his glasses. She kicked Rose hard. Ash joined in the laughter.

"Never you idiot, he is my protector, always my big brother," Menaka replied. Dylan's face fell. He knew Menaka looked on him as an elder brother and guardian, even a chaperone. Menaka's mother, Manel Fernando, had cursed him with this label and responsibility when they were neighbours, and it had stuck. She knew he was responsible and above all decent. He hated his decency now.

"Well if you do decide to, me and Ash could be your bridesmaid and best man, we promise, just think about it."

Rose loved baiting Menaka, but this time Menaka refused to bite and looked away. Dylan promptly re-adopted his nodding off routine. She was wrapped up like an Eskimo – parka, beanie and a woolen jacket against the cold, but he could still see her elegance and poise through it all.

"Damn! I wish the weather was clear, Orion's Belt should appear very clearly these days," Ash said with some frustration. He was a self-taught astronomer who owned a very expensive telescope sent by his sister who lived in Melbourne. His tree hut was both an adventurous getaway and an ill-equipped observatory.

"Are you crazy? Look down and see if you can spot that Yakush, that would be like winning the lottery."Rose was about to giggle again.

"Mass in a few more hours, wish I had slept."

Dylan moaned. Both Dylan and Ashwin went to Sunday mass, their parents made sure of that.

"Piano lessons for me," Menaka said with a very graphic twinkle in her eyes. Dylan hated her piano tutor, who he had never seen. Ash and Rose exchanged looks and suffered a relapse of laughter.

"Well I have a debating class, rehearsals for the Saraswati dance and a prefect meeting; shall we meet at our place in the afternoon, to decide what's next, after 12?"Rose did everything, they did not know how.

Dylan almost fell off the tree house and Menaka screamed as it shook from a massive blow. Rose and Ashwin looked terrified but held their cool.

"What is it? Will it climb up?" Menaka had turned pale.

The tree shook again, more violently this time. Suddenly there was chaos at the foot of the tree, the gloat bleating and the ground shaking violently. Rose recovered her nerves and directed the flashlight down. Suddenly two dark shapes scrambled out of the mist.

"There! There!" Rose yelled.

They looked very familiar, like… like cows – stray cattle from a nearby farm. They laughed out loud. The goat annoyingly continued to kick a fuss.

"Ok guys I'm dying to get some sleep, nothing's going to happen now, let's go." Ash sounded the retreat after two more hours. The others agreed drowsily.

This was their third weekend on the watch, and they had upgraded their effort with the live bait. They were getting tired. They had spent sleepless nights and suffered borderline frostbite. Wearily, they climbed down the ladder in single file. It was four fifteen; they could feel the dawn stirring and the night departing. Ash, who was the first down, let out a war whoop and pointed stupidly at the base of the tree with his flashlight.

"Hey, hey guys look!"

Joy was stamped on his face – it scared the others more. The old goat had vanished into thin air, or the mist. Rose joined in the celebrations. Dylan kicked off his exhaustion and began recording the broken cord that had held the goat with his camcorder, its generous meal of Jak leaves still scattered about. Menaka was close to tears.

"Poor thing."

She had been half hoping that their innocent bait would live to tell the tale to its grandkids. But that was not to be.

"Hey! Do you think it's still out here somewhere? I can't see a thing through this stupid…"

Rose couldn't finish, Menaka screamed and Dylan was half way up the ladder. Dylan wanted to kill Rose as she collapsed in a fit holding her sides.

"I could kill you for that." Menaka gave Rose a smart slap on her back, but the affectionate violence hardly left a mark on her aggressive humour. Ash couldn't help joining her, the contagion of mirth too much to resist.

"Now we'll have to pay Muruga uncle at least three thousand rupees for the goat." Rose brought up the practical cost of their so-called success, still holding her sides. Muruga uncle measured his modest wealth in a herd of goats and three cows.

Dylan was silent as he escorted Menaka home, apparently absorbed in the light from his torch, which was struggling against the thick mist.

"What's the problem, are you tired?" Menaka disrupted the drought of words.

Dylan shrugged.

"Just a headache," he lied and looked down. He looked as if he was in pain, more like he was hurt.

"Can I give you some paracetamol when we get home?"

Menaka was mothering him. He loved it. They were passing the old British Cemetery where the bones of men, women, children and babies from over two centuries of colonial rule rested. He could feel her body pressing against his; he knew she was scared. He cautiously pressed her against him with a protective arm. She got even closer. He was worried that she might feel his racing pulse.

They soon reached her house.

"Could you please *please* call me when you get home?" Menaka begged.

Dylan shrugged his shoulders and turned back, enjoying every bit of it. He knew he had to pass the cemetery again, which was a killjoy even at this hour when most of humanity was still immersed in sleep. With the sign of the cross he broke in to a sprint near the cemetery, hurriedly reciting the Lord's Prayer as he did. He got home and prepared for bed, keeping a hawk-eye on his mobile. He didn't call. His heart stopped as the phone rang. He smiled and answered it.

"You idiot, I asked you to call didn't I? I was worried."

She sounded furious.

"Sorry, I forgot."

He laughed as she banged down the phone.

SHE TOUCHED HER MOTHER'S FEET

CHAPTER 2
ANOTHER SUNDAY

Dylan was interested in mass for a change – it was a brand new priest and he was refreshingly young. Ash didn't care; he was checking out the scene or the chicks, which was all the same to him. Most of his 'innocent flings', as he so irritatingly put it, had had their origins in Sunday mass. The old priest, who bored half the parish with his marathon and highly irrelevant sermons every Sunday, lolled on a back bench in the pulpit. The hard-hitting and furiously delivered theme rolled over the church, grabbing the short-lived attention span of most parishioners. It was about living the faith, and the priest came down harshly on 'checklist Christians' who confined their obligations merely to Sunday mass and other social activities.

"Help the poor, not in words but with kindness and ACTIONS," he boomed, licking his lips as they ran dry.

Dylan desperately hoped that his parents would take note. He saw his father, Rex Perera, idiotically wiping away an imaginary fleck of dust off his brand new pants and his mother, Dorothy, reciting the rosary like a parrot, silently. They were staunch Catholics and even stronger hypocrites. They were typical checklist Christians.

They disliked Dylan's friendship with Rose because she was from a minority group, a Hindu, and above all poor. Dylan had risen in vain against their hypocrisy.

"Why do you go to church at all if you can't live even the basics, didn't god say 'blessed are the poor'?" he had come back at his mother.

"Don't try to preach to me ok?" she had roared pompously, loud enough to bring the roof down.

"That girl has nothing, she could be a gold digger. She knows you are loaded, they will do anything to latch themselves on to someone with wealth."

"What! Are you serious?"

Dylan was too shocked to feel offended. Rose loved the world, not anything material in it. And she was his friend; he had no other interest in her. They were just teenagers, marriage was a mythical and distant concept for him. If only she knew who owned his real affections.

"That girl is the most selfless…" he had started, but gave up. They wouldn't understand or accept the existence of people who loved life and the world about them without wanting to own it. She judged the world by her own standards.

"You people will never understand." He had got up, pushing the chair back with a loud noise.

"What's that, what is he saying?" His father, short in height and more pompous even than his mother had stuck his head out from his study. That was the last thing Dylan wanted.

"He wants to teach us our religion," Dorothy had said, making a sarcastic face.

"Don't you bloody talk to your mother like that ever again, if we talked to our parents like that they would have whacked us, seventeen or not. We give you everything, so be grateful and drop your attitude."

He had locked himself in his room and shaken his mood with his PS3 and his movies. He hated his status as an only child; the expectations were unbearable. They wanted to sacrifice him to fulfill all their unfulfilled aspirations. His father was the senior accountant in a leading private firm. His mother was a teacher, who applied her unduly harsh discipline, honed at school with tender loving care, at home as well. He extended his pity to her students. They wanted to make a nice lawyer or doctor out of him.

"Both those fields are tougher than accounting, why does he want me to go above him when he himself got off easily as an accountant?" he had drilled his mother one day.

"Because your cousin is a doctor and his sister is a lawyer, and you know that Francis uncle was only a book keeper, so his kids have outshone their parents. If they could do it why can't you?"

"But, but Mummy each person is different, I am different, my passion is journalism."

Dylan was drained by the total absence of logic in her argument. He hated his two older cousins, even though it was never their fault.

"Journalism! Journalism!" Dorothy croaked. "I'll tell you right now, your Daddy will disown you before you even talk about it, how would you ever feed your family from a journalist's salary you fool?" She was getting loud again. She was always loud.

"So journalists starve do they?" Dylan countered with a sinking feeling. He had already concluded that they lacked the capacity for any reason. Perhaps God had created them that way. He even hated calling them *Daddy* and *Mummy*. They had forced it on him when he was very young. They dressed and ate, with fork and spoon, just like the Suddhas or British as they were called, and this after almost seventy years of independence. They were proud victims of the colonial hangover. Ash called his parents *Father* and *Mother* in proper traditional fashion. Dylan was embarrassed when some of the kids from Primary taunted him over it. His partner in pain was Menaka. She was missing something at home as well, she wasn't too sure what it was unlike him, she thought it was trust. Her father, Yasantha, had diverted his affections to a pretty thing from Colombo when she was just twelve. Dylan had seen her, and Menaka suspected that she was still in her late twenties. Manel aunty had brought them up alone since then; her younger brother Devon was ten.

"She never trusts me I... I feel, I have never ever let her down with anything like other girls, she should know that by now, she wants to know where I am or what I am doing every minute, she is like a... like a watchdog," Menaka had told him one day.

She didn't sound too devastated. And there was no reason to, he thought. But he had enough wisdom not to share it with her.

"I feel smothered sometimes, and need a break. I feel like doing something actually bad just to prove a point sometimes, you know? But that's not me either," she said with her shy smile. Dylan trembled deliciously as he heard the 'bad' bit. Manel aunty never allowed her to go anywhere unescorted. He was the only guy who enjoyed that rare privilege, and he hated it.

"You want to swap with mine? You will worship your mother after that," Dylan said. Menaka had laughed.

"My parents are open books, they could be read by anyone with a brain slightly larger than a chickpea," was his prognosis. Rose and Ash had laughed until they cried when they heard it.

"That was a fantastic sermon wasn't it?" Lionel De Alwis, Ashwin's father, handsome, tall and rich, asked Rex with a genial smile. He punched Dylan gently in the ribs. Dylan loved Lionel uncle and Florence aunty – they were loaded, but down to earth. Florence aunty: short, roly-poly and kind, loved Rose. Rose's mother Meena had at one time been employed in their tea estate, but they obviously did not believe in class and social distinction. They were happy with Ash's friendship with the vivacious Rose.

"Yes… yes superb," Dylan's Father lied as his mother smiled idiotically at Florence.

"Young priest, no? He must have definitely fooled around before he joined the seminary, he looks a bit *playboy-ish* still doesn't he?" His mother had finally opened her mouth. Dylan wanted the ground to swallow him up. Florence smiled with quiet resignation.

"So did you catch the Yakush yesterday son?" Lionel uncle asked with a kind smile.

"What stupidity, no? Instead of studying at home they waste their time, and in this freezing weather; this idiot suffers from the wheeze sometimes and needs the puffer." Rex pointed at Dylan.

"Ah, but we were that age too weren't we? If they don't do these things now, then when? I had better fun than these jokers, let them enjoy their monster," Lionel rebuffed Dylan's father mildly but firmly.

Rex Perera squirmed uncomfortably and went to get his expensive car. Rex had taken a massive loan to buy his brand new Outlander, from the very first batch imported in. He had threatened Ash to get him in to the vehicle two days after he had bought it. Ash had wanted to stay behind for soccer and there was a slight drizzle.

"No way! You are not playing in this weather."

He had suffered a lecture on all its super cool features under duress. Rex had added an extra 20 minutes to their journey home.

"Hey what time at Rose's?" Ash's eyelids were half closed.

"After twelve, let's give Menaka time to finish her stupid piano class," Dylan whispered with some venom in his tone.

"Ok, see you then."

Dylan watched wistfully as Ashwin departed with his parents.

Menaka's class was running late. The two boys lazed outside; the sun was out in force and a delicious wind swept down from the high plains challenging the budding heat.

"Shall we go and sit inside?" Ash suggested.

"No, I don't want to," Dylan was adamant.

"Why not?"

Before Dylan could answer, the door opened and a young guy stepped outside, Menaka following him. Dylan's heart stopped for a moment. He had never seen Priyantha before, just heard about him from Menaka's verbal diarrhea. He was fair complexioned and looked quite dashing in a casual t-shirt and jeans. Clean-shaven, with finely chiseled cheeks and chin, hair swept back, and with a super fit body, he could have easily passed as a very close blood relative of Hamid Khan, the Bollywood superstar. She had not been exaggerating. He had desperately hoped she had been.

Priyantha was a young, unemployed graduate with an Economics degree, and a piano prodigy. His reputation had spread by word of mouth and Manel aunty had asked him to tutor Menaka on the piano. She had killed two birds with one stone, providing him with an income and getting her lessons, all under the protective comfort of their home.

"I'll see you next Sunday, practice those notes ok?"

He was extremely soft spoken, and had a kind smile.

"Ok sir." Menaka was all smiles. Dylan had never seen her smile that long at a stretch. His breath came in fits and starts. Priyantha smiled cordially at the two boys as he strapped on his helmet.

"Hey, do you love him as much as I do?" Menaka broke into Dylan's concentration as he kept looking at Priyantha's departing bike.

"Yeah right."

Dylan looked angrily at her and Menaka's face immediately collapsed into an apology.

"Dylan, please bring her back by two, ok son?" Manel aunty's stern but kindly face appeared at the doorway.

"Ok aunty, " he replied meekly, with a sinking feeling. Ash looked away to hide his smile. He didn't want to rub it in as well. Menaka sprinted back to her mother and touched her feet.

"Budu Saranai: May the Buddha Bless You."

Manel's eyes swam in affection as she stroked her daughter's head ever so delicately, giving her blessings with the fullness of her heart. Dylan couldn't get over it, his admiration. She was steeped in good old-fashioned tradition; touching the feet of her mother to receive her blessings before stepping out of the house was an act of reverence taught in Buddhist philosophy.

Menaka was wearing a simple pink top and a knee length cotton skirt with her favourite floral design – a spray of pink, yellow and orange flowers. Half her wardrobe was filled with the same pastoral theme. Dylan made a pathetic effort to un-rivet his eyes from its simple glory.

"Where were you? I thought you would never come," Rose asked as they reached her house, blowing the tedious strand of hair from her face. "Did Menaka's boyfriend hold you guys back?" Rose knew how to play Dylan. Dylan gave her the same look and she understood, she saw the pain too.

They loved Rose's house, mostly because the family was always happy and some of it rubbed off on them. They had only a fraction of what Dylan, Ash and Menaka had materially, but they more than made up for it in emotional well-being. Their house was near a trickle of water that came from a pipe on the mountain, their meagre front yard was always spotlessly clean, and a giant breadfruit tree stood majestically in the middle, towering over a cute wooden seat made by Rose's father. Meena, Rose's mother and Thanga, her father, were just too hospitable. They had just moved in to this new house, which didn't even have a heater for the cold nights. Meena was a hunched young woman; hard work had hidden her good looks and deformed her original posture. She now worked in the tea grading section at the Labookel estate. Thanga worked in a nearby Aluminum factory.

Ashwin, Dylan and Menaka had tried desperately to stop them from attaching the *Master* and *Miss* tags whenever they addressed them. Master Ashwin, Master Dylan or Miss Menaka, this was undeserving and deferential treatment from two individuals who wrongly believed that they belonged to the lower social classes in society. Generations of incorrect social norms and treatment had forced them into this needless subservience. Dylan and Ashwin had threatened to walk out one day if they didn't call them by their names, and Meena had looked tearful. But nothing had changed. Rose didn't care.

Rose's seven-year-old brother Raju was playing, shirtless, with his friends. He loved playing marbles. Menaka called him and gave him two chocolate bars. His joy lit up his face, and they immediately stopped their game and shared the rich treat in total harmony.

"So what now?" Rose was itching to get on with it.

Dylan, who was still sulking, warmed to the subject with a tentative smile.

"We must go to Bakers Falls; some of the sightings including that attack have been near there, otherwise we will be wasting our time, isn't it?"

"Sounds like a plan," Menaka agreed with a smile. Dylan glowed and looked up to see her large black eyes swimming in his. Shy as he was, he held the gaze for an eternity, which was what thirty seconds felt like.

Rose winked at Ash. They kept quiet.

"World's End is easy to reach, but Bakers Falls is a harder route, are you sure about the path? I've only been with my father," Ash asked Dylan.

"No you're right, damn! I am not sure either."

Dylan scratched his head. World's End was a spectacularly sheer drop of 1050m at one end of Horton Plains, and one could see the entire countryside rolling below.

"Got an idea," Rose said, blowing in to her face again. They could see the light bulbs exploding in her brain. "You know that little guy who said he was attacked near Bakers Falls? I know where his family lives. I will try to tempt him to come. He should know the area like the back of his hand. His name is Sindhu."

"Fantastic! Great! Let's do it next Friday then. It's a public holiday for the Poya full moon, what do you say?"

There was an excited agreement – only Menaka looked doubtful.

"I don't think mother will agree," she said with a worried look.

"I will get you permission – if you are not going, we are not going, ok? That's final," Dylan spoke up with unexpected enthusiasm and sprightly conviction. Menaka looked at him again with gratitude. Rose got up and saluted Dylan smartly. Even he couldn't resist it this time.

The silence happened between them again. Ash went to the school grounds to play soccer with his friends and Dylan took up his designated place next to Menaka. He scavenged for the scoring dialogue, but the more he tried the muter he became.

"Hope the weather's good next Friday." Menaka finally broke the spell. Dylan was grateful.

"Let's go anyway, we won't get another chance," Dylan said, his confidence rallying.

"I still have this nasty feeling that my mother might say no."

"Remember we won't go without you, so I will somehow get her permission," Dylan said, with a shy glance at her.

"Aha, you might be right, she might not say no to my guardian," Menaka said.

"What a curse," Dylan muttered.

"Sorry, what did you say?"

"That's good, if she does," Dylan backpedalled quickly.

"Lucky it's not on a Sunday," Menaka said.

"WHY?"

Dylan's tone shocked him more than what Menaka was suggesting.

"No, just that I would hate to miss my piano lesson, he is sooo dedicated."

"Really?" Dylan said with a pretend yawn. Menaka laughed suddenly.

"Why did you laugh?"

Dylan wasn't sure whether she'd caught it or not.

"No no, you sound so tired, perhaps you need your beauty sleep after yesterday?"

"Yes I am, what a waste that was," Dylan said. "I don't want to repeat that every weekend, I was really bored."

"Oh, I loved it, perhaps we were boring company for you?" Menaka sounded hurt. She was smiling as she looked away.

Dylan wanted to kick himself.

"No, no, no you are never boring, not even if you tried, that's the only plus with all that,"

Dylan stammered. She smiled.

"Thanks, that's very sweet. You will make a very romantic boyfriend one day. Have you ever had a crush on a girl, really?"

"I never had, but… but now I do, just haven't got the guts to ask her." Dylan was going from strength to strength.

"Who? Who? Have I seen her? Please tell me! Wow you kept a lid on that didn't you? Which school does she go to?"

Menaka was excited. Dylan toyed with the idea of telling her the name of the school, but didn't want to make it obvious.

"Hmmm, that's a secret."

"Do I... do I know her?" Menaka couldn't stop.

"P-perhaps."

"WHO? C'mon, please tell me, why haven't you asked her yet?"

"I don't want to lose her trust, she respects me now," he said with grave misgivings. He didn't want to blow it.

"What a waste, perhaps she is desperate for you to tell her as well, you and your stupid pessimism, she'll find someone else soon, you wait and see."

She exposed the unsavoury risk. Dylan was filled with self-loathing, wishing she could see the truth.

"Ow!" Menaka clutched her ankle in pain, losing her balance. Dylan propped her up easily.

"Are you ok?" Dylan bent to touch her ankle, but didn't follow through, too scared that she might be offended.

"What a guy, doesn't even check if his friend's ankle is broken or not."

She sounded annoyed. Dylan dropped on his knees in a flash, his heart making him deaf, hands vibrating, and lifted her ankle like a fragile ornament. Menaka balanced herself with one hand on his back. He rubbed his palms together vigorously, blew in to them and massaged her ankle softly. He was drenched in tense joy. She gingerly replaced her ankle back into her leather sandal.

"Wow! You've got gifted hands, good as new, where did you learn that from?"

"Oh! From the TV, saw a Shaolin Priest do it." Dylan barely heard his own voice.

"Wish you could do it on the other ankle as well," Menaka said wistfully. Dylan was back on his knees in a flash, his back hunched.

"I was joking silly, but thanks."

He didn't hear anything else she said until they reached her house.

Sindhu lived in poor estate line house, which was a house smashed against five or six more sitting in one row, like match boxes pasted together. Rose loved him the moment she saw him. He was a little guy with a winning smile and cleanly shaven head, due to a Hindu vow, Rose knew.

"Hey little brother," Rose called him, and immediately slipped three chocolate bars that Menaka had given her into his hand. He almost fell off the broken swing that he was seated on.

"Oooh Taaank Youuu." His eyes bulged out.

"Do you go to school?" Rose asked.

"Nooo," he replied, as if offended. It was a luxury for them.

"How old are you?" Rose was curious.

"Eight," he said.

"Hey, is it true that you were attacked by that Yakush near Bakers Falls, when you were bathing with your friends?" Rose approached the topic.

"Yeah." He sounded offended again, as if anyone should ever doubt him. He was the local superstar.

"Did you get any wounds by…" Rose couldn't finish.

He lifted his torn vest and proudly showed his back. Rose hooted with laughter. She laughed so much that her stomach hurt and she ended up choking and crying at the same time.

"Hey! Why are you laughing like that, what's so funny?" Sindhu was furious.

"That… that's a…. scratch… did, did that thing dooo it?" Rose could hardly speak through her laughter as she pointed to the battle-scarred cat that was calmly washing itself below the swing. Sindhu picked up a pebble to hit her. Rose held up her hand in peace, still laughing.

"Nooo, it was this big monster with a massive tail and glowing eyes, I went down for a dive and…" He was settling in for the heroics.

"Hey! Can you lead us to Bakers Falls next Friday, if you're free? We don't know how to get there. I will give you a gift that you won't forget in hurry, what do you say?"

Rose did not have time for the details. Sindhu did a sudden handstand on the ground.

"I am in," he yelled.

"Ok, then come by our place by six in the morning ok? I will remind you closer to the day, don't sleep late, exactly six ok?"

Rose gave him the directions.

She gave him an affectionate pat on his bald head before leaving. She wasn't so sure about Bakers Falls anymore.

On the way back she took a more scenic and adventurous short cut that passed through Hunas Falls and Muruga uncle's farm. His herd of goats and three cows were grazing in the pasture below. She saw the old goat with the long and short horns leading the pack proudly with its kids and grandkids. She laughed out loud. She was desperate to tax the Prof further on the mystery of the missing goat, and she wanted to share its ultimate salvation with Menaka as soon as she met her next. At least they had saved three thousand rupees. She was smiling all the way home.

ON THE TRAIL

CHAPTER 3
ON THE TRAIL

"Hey! Shall we visit World's End first? The weather's looking good, I think we could go to Bakers Falls from there right, and that's the official story we have given anyway. What do you think?"

"Let's do it, why not? I can't remember the last time I went there, but I have never looked down."

Menaka was unstoppable – she didn't care where they went as long as it was away from home. She just wanted to flee maternal suffocation. Dylan had pulled it off and got permission for her to join them on their 'project', as he had delicately referred to it. But no one had mentioned Bakers Falls, since it was off the beaten track.

"Now look who's talking," Rose said with her signature smile and blowing the ever-present strand of hair away from her face.

Menaka had collapsed in a fit of laughter when Rose related the return of the old goat a few days before. Dylan was not so amused; he'd thought he had something there. Ash was already spreading his arms wide and sucking in the fresh air, just like his father had always taught him to do. It was a special place at a special hour, filled with the refreshing music of the forest at the break of dawn.

"The air over here is priceless, just spread your arms wide and suck it in, it is a natural healer."

His father had elaborated on all their walks together. But the happiest was Sindhu. He had arrived at 4.30am, and Rose was still groggy with sleep.

Menaka had already given him the thousand-rupee note that was reserved for the end of his labours. Rose had wanted to choke her; the agreed amount was five hundred, and another five hundred as a surprise sweetener, all at the end. Ash, Dylan and Menaka had pooled in their pocket money.

"Don't you dare give him anything at the start, or else he might vanish with it even before we begin."

Rose had been quite specific in her warning. Menaka had taken it in one ear and spat it out the other in one seamless stream. She loved the little kid and found his hardships hard to take. He now followed her like a lost puppy and did his best to show off and steal her attention. The unending handstands and loud whistling that echoed back from the wilderness had finally gotten to Ash.

"Hey, you are going to lead ok?" He had grabbed Sindhu firmly by the shoulders and pulled him to the front. Menaka giggled.

"Sin, please stop it," she said, meaning it was a sin to do that to him.

Dylan and Ash had come armed to the teeth. Dylan had his trusty camcorder and powerful binoculars, while Ash had brought along his pricey digital Polaroid camera. They had their mobile phones and the torches. They wore tough mountain boots and were rugged up in expensive jumpers and beanies. They had also brought their towels and swimming trunks in their backpacks for a dip in Bakers Falls, which they had never done. Rose wore a jumper and pants from the wardrobe Ash's mother had gifted her over the years, and Sindhu just had a dirty T-shirt, shorts and slippers on. Dylan lagged behind; he wanted to keep an eye out for the rich birdlife that saturated the area and, more importantly, admire Menaka at leisure. She was dressed in a colourful pullover and wore comfortable jeans and tall boots. Her backpack contained an assortment of her mother's signature Chinese rolls, vegetable cutlets, spicy tuna sandwiches and homemade pomegranate juice.

They made a brief stopover at the famous Hanuman Kovil along the way. It was almost 6.30am and it was empty, except for the Poosari, the holy man in charge who was worshipping the gods with incense. He smiled at the group while Rose worshipped and forced Sindhu to do the same; it was the last thing on his mind.

The larger-than-life statue of the monkey god Hanuman looked down on them, a benign gaze etched on its features. Legend had it that Hanuman was sent by the Indian king Rama to rescue his queen, Seetha, who was taken away by Ravana, yet another king made famous by his legendary amour, a story immortalised in the epic *Ramayanaya*. The Kovil was right on the banks of a pretty river, which spread the feeling of serenity and peace.

Dylan was soon reeling out the names of all the birds that crossed his binoculars: Flameback, Whistling Thrush and the Kashmir Flycatcher were among those he spotted. Langur monkeys became daring and cheekier as they left the last of the human habitation behind. A flying squirrel startled them as it flew low overhead. Menaka held her breath, eyes transfixed on its flight. But it was the reserved and graceful Paradise Flycatcher, with a long white tail like a bridal veil, that really caught her fancy. There was no sign of the obsessively shy and nervous sambar.

"Hey Prof! Have you seen the Pigheaded Blue Tit anywhere?" Ash asked Dylan in scholarly earnestness after putting up with an eternity of name-calling.

"Never heard of that..." Dylan started, then picked up a rock to throw at Ash when he realised that it was made up. Rose squealed with laughter. Menaka turned her face away to hide her giggles. Sindhu laughed the loudest, not understanding anything. They lost track of time as they absorbed their surroundings at a languid pace.

Suddenly, as if divided by a fine line drawn in invisible paint, the forest stopped and the plains commenced, gently undulating land covered with giant Patana grass and dwarf trees as far as the eye could see. An expansive ocean of greenery, a limitless tabletop propped up by mountains. They stopped, the scenery possessing them all for a moment. Streams and mini lakes shimmered in the late morning sun. Dylan, Ash and the girls knew that three of the biggest rivers in the land started their journey somewhere out there. To the east, at least twenty kilometres away towards the lower end of the plains, was Ashwin's tea estate with the tree hut. It was a much longer route and they had taken a short cut.

"Wow! Do you ever get tired of looking at this?" Ash finally found his tongue, but no one bothered to reply, the landscape still controlling their faculties. Even Sindhu was strangely silent, his inspiration for the silence a mystery.

They walked through the grass for another hour and a bit, and soon the wind picked up with force as they emerged on the narrow rocky ledge at the End of the World. The skies were still a cheerful blue with plenty of cloud cover. The mist had surprisingly departed, allowing them to feast and treat their eyes. There was a solitary tree that looped over the edge.

Sindhu made a beeline to the tree and looked down at the delicious terror below, cool as anything.

"You idiot come back here! Rose! Ask that idiot to get back from the edge please."

Menaka was clutching her heart and doubling up in anticipation of an imminent fall over the deep end. Rose laughed and casually joined Sindhu at the tree, looking down at the world at her feet.

"You crazy show offs." Menaka resorted to insults, but the pair didn't budge. Dylan was dying to escort Menaka to the edge and give her a taste of wonder and awe, but he had to get over his own vertigo first.

"Could you hold my boots and we'll take turns looking down?" Dylan whispered in Ash's ear. He was struck by Rose and Sindhu's callous disregard for their safety.

"Ok," Ash supported the plan meekly. Dylan trembled over to the edge first, on all fours, his boots safely anchored in Ash's hands. Then it was Ash's turn. Their breathing vied against the mournful sound of the high winds.

"Oh! You two chickens." Rose's comment ate into their bones. Sindhu, true to form, laughed loudest.

"Menaka, please you need to see this," Dylan volunteered out of fear and love.

"No way, noooooo."

"What! Are you crazy? You can't miss it again, trust us and hold our hands; we will never let you fall." Rose was the picture of assurance, and she motioned Sindhu towards Menaka.

"No, no." Menaka was adamant, but caved in as she felt Rose and Sindhu propping her up with firm grips.

They gingerly supported her to the tree; she was drowning in sweat. She took a split second peek and screamed.

"Enough! Enough! I saw."

Rose and Sindhu pulled her back gently and she flopped on the ground, exhausted. Dylan couldn't get over the wasted opportunity.

"Wow! That was awesome, thanks," Menaka whispered.

"Reeaaally?" Rose adopted an, 'I told you so' stance.

"Oh! Look at that." Menaka pointed a trembling finger at the rock surface near the foot of the tree.

We will leap together and finally be united in love, no one can separate us now, Dawson and Mona, 1945.

The writing of the desperate lovers stood out clearly, etched in stone for all posterity. They were all immersed in a moment of reflection, except for Sindhu, who was smiling uncontrollably. Menaka struggled to acknowledge the spectre of death amid such breathtaking beauty.

"Ok, let's go to Bakers Falls, it's getting late," Ash said after more than half an hour at the Edge. It was almost eleven in the morning. Sindhu, sure-footed and agile, took the lead. It was a descent this time, and over much more slippery terrain. Ferns, moss and grass drenched in a perpetual coating of moisture tested their balance with every step. Menaka was worst hit; Dylan positioned himself strategically to offer a helping hand, but his noble intentions were compromised by his awkward agility.

"So, who is helping who here?" Rose said, witnessing the comedy of errors. Dylan was too tired to feel embarrassed. After more than two hours they could hear a faint gurgling sound that gradually gathered volume. They got over a ridge and saw the waterfall. It was a body of pure white water that cascaded gracefully over a series of rocks, creating several rocky pools. It was one of the jewels in Horton Plains and a famous watering hole for the sambar, the leopard, the bear and the mischievous langur monkeys. They knew that the more notorious heavyweights ventured out at night. Ash and Dylan got in to their swimming trunks and gingerly dipped their toes in the water. Dylan handed his glasses over to Menaka.

"Ohhh! This is, like, freezing."

Dylan was suddenly uncertain about his ambitions to bathe; Ash remained tight-lipped, sharing his concern. Suddenly Dylan screamed as a spray of icy cold water drenched him. Sindhu had splashed some water over him.

"I'll kill you, you crazy monke..."

Dylan got up mad, but he felt a pair of hands push him in to the water. It was Rose this time.

The shock numbed his body. He heard a muffled cry as Ash joined him. The numbness soon passed as their bodies adjusted to the below zero temperatures. Sindhu was about to take off his t-shirt when Rose pinched his ear and dragged him back.

"Just what do you think you are going to wear when you come out?"

He smiled sheepishly and sat on bent knees, looking sadly at the two boys. Menaka slid an arm around him with a sympathetic smile.

"You should have brought your swimming things you know, there is no one here," Dylan yelled out through clashing teeth, half looking at Menaka. Menaka gave him a wry look that said it all; even Rose struggled with some cultural reservations when it came to swimming with the boys in the open.

Ash and Dylan ate the lion's share of Aunty Manel's rolls and sandwiches with unstinted assistance from Sindhu. Rose demolished the vegetarian cutlets. The waters and the weary trek had taken their toll on their appetites. It felt unreal for Ash and Dylan as they ate, dipped in the waters and ate again. Their mission was lost in the moment.

"Hey look!" Rose called out and pointed around with some concern. A white aerial squall was moving in from all sides, occupying an ever-decreasing area of light. But it was worse than just mist; they saw dark clouds joining ranks with the white veil. A notorious highland storm was closing in fast, the first flashes of lightning in the distance. They knew that up here things could get real nasty, real fast. The lightning had a reputation as a killer; innocent farmers and their families got struck by lightning with unreasonable regularity.

The boys got in to their dry clothes in no time, their teeth clashing against each other and bodies shivering with a combination of cold and fear. Dylan fumbled with his glasses as he put them back on. The group meekly fell behind Sindhu to lead the way, but he was displaying very unconvincing confidence this time. He reluctantly gave in to his underrated reputation with a courageous, "This way," took a deep breath and turned in to the gathering gloom. Dylan quickly produced the torches, then the sheet of rain that they had seen in the distance burst on them, coming down hard, in buckets.

"Look! Look! Over there."

Sindhu suddenly stood stock-still and began pointing his torch wildly at the ground. The others were terrified and followed his gaze, struggling to focus in the fragile light. Ash let out a gasp. It was a gigantic print, obviously not human and freshly made.

"That's a paw print," Dylan said ecstatically. They all knew that it was bigger than anything a normal creature could have made. "Perhaps it's still out there."

Dylan looked around, fear radiating through his water logged glasses. Menaka promptly shared his viewpoint and threw nervous glances all over the place. She was oozing sweat. Rose leapt into action and pulled the camera from Ash's hands, desperate to net this vital piece of evidence. A growl quickly halted her movement. It was up close and personal. Now it was Menaka's turn to scream, but the noise knotted itself and fell from her throat. Dylan pressed his hand gently over her mouth and gestured madly with his face.

SHE HELD HIM ON HER LAP

CHAPTER 4
THE LOST SOUL'S
GRAVEYARD

The leopard was just meters away, a full-grown specimen with an arrogant snarl etched on its face. Raindrops bounced off its bright yellow, dotted hide. Menaka trembled like a leaf against Dylan's chest. He felt a strange calm as he held her. Ash was frozen, Sindhu just sat on the ground, and they could all hear Rose breathing hard.

It stood motionless and majestic, unfazed by them. Then with an expression that looked like a sarcastic smile, it faded back in to the trees and the billowing mist. The print on the ground was a thing of the past; they heard only their hearts racing as they ran for it, their torches barely illuminating the ground ahead of them.

Soon they hit a clearing; the storm was showing signs of letting up. Thunder still rolled overhead, but there was a pinprick of light somewhere in the heavens, between the peaks. The time spelt impending doom – it was four-forty and they knew that any light would be snuffed out pretty quickly as the highland dusk settled in at its leisure. Sindhu was the first to drop, doubled up with exhaustion. They took his cue and flopped on the ground, panting like dogs.

"I have never seen one, not one," he gushed.

"And you have been attacked by the monster you say, never seen a leopard," Rose said, slapping his shaven head affectionately.

"Damn! I wish I'd taken a photo, that was awesome. I never dreamt I would see one outside of Yala." Ash found his speech between mouthfuls of air. He had seen some rare leopards when they visited the Yala Wildlife Sanctuary with his family – it had an international reputation for high leopard numbers.

"I thought he might have had us for dinner, I thought they'd be terrified of us, but he didn't budge." Dylan expressed everyone's relief. Menaka was strangely silent.

"You ok?" Dylan rubbed her shoulders gently. They were both trembling now, more from the cold this time.

"I d-d-don't kn-know about the leopard, but my mother will k-kill me," she stammered. Dylan gave her shoulders a tight squeeze.

"Don't worry I'll take the fall, she's really not that bad." Dylan was all assurance, and Menaka smiled gratefully.

"Shall we go? It looks like some kind of trail here, this might lead us somewhere."

Ash wearily got up and the others followed. They knew that Sindhu was well and truly lost. They also knew it was not his fault.

Ash took the lead, his torchlight not giving away anything. The rain had reduced to a drizzle but the mist had compensated for its loss. They were drenched, but strangely their bodies had decided to ignore it. They had walked for another hour and a bit when Sindhu suddenly executed a terrifying tumble over something. They didn't expect him to walk after that, but he was remarkably resilient and got up in almost the same breath. Rose and Menaka were all over him, dusting the dirt off and checking for any life threatening injuries.

"No, I am ok," he said with an easy smile, not wanting the fuss. His right knee was bleeding slightly, with the skin scraped off. Mother Nature had made him for this; it was the unspoken truth.

They looked closely at the obstacle, and Sindhu gasped – it was a gravestone. To their horror he started crying uncontrollably, fear distorting his innocent features.

"The Lost Soul's graveyard, the Lost Soul's graveyard." He repeated the name like a mantra. Menaka quickly rushed to his side and hugged him, almost carrying him in her arms. Sindhu gave in to her attention and compassion, still sobbing. They all knew why he had got scared. Even Rose looked a bit off colour, a rare thing for her. The Lost Soul's graveyard was the final resting place of notorious murderers and criminals who had over the centuries preyed on the innocent from the cold depths of the forest and the plains. Superstitious villagers found it terrifying even during the day. Ghosts had been spotted of both murderer and victim. The gravestones were covered with vines and grass, unnamed and neglected for very good reason.

"Hey Sindhu! Look, see, ghosts are harmless things, we are scarier and more brutal than ghosts ok?" Ash shared this simple and honest philosophy with him. He knew enough about the infinite pain his species were capable of inflicting on their own. They could see a flicker of his usual smile breaking across Sindhu's face. Menaka cuddled him closer.

The rain had ceased and the night had arrived, they were stranded in the middle of a cemetery with a bad reputation, and they had simply stopped there, common sense taking over, knowing that further progress in the dark was useless. They had only one option left, and that was dawn and daylight. They all sat wherever they could, and it was soggy wherever they sat. Ash, Dylan and Menaka rested their backs against the broken headstones with no names. The mist was still strong. Dylan tried his mobile phone continuously with a sinking feeling, knowing that at this height there was no signal.

"What was that?" Rose's ears perked to attention like a sniffer dog.

"What stupido, we hear nooothing." Ash pulled her leg.

"Perhaps it's a ghooost," he said, waving his arms scarily over her. Rose ignored him and continued her concentrated listening. They all heard it then, a sobbing sound, growing louder and louder, then running footsteps, twigs snapping noisily, closer now. Ash screamed as something hit them. The apparition screamed louder; they couldn't move. Sindhu yelled in pain as Menaka pressed his ribs in a deadly grip. The ghost was a child, covered in scratches and gasping for breath. Tears rained freely down her cheeks. The rain had soaked her to the bones and she was trembling like a leaf. Her white garment was plastered on to her painfully thin frame. She looked sweet.

"Please! Please! Help me they are coming after me." She began to sob even louder.

"Who? Who is coming?" Ash took charge and held her face in his palms, wiping her tears gently with his thumbs. The child's breathing slowed down.

'They... they are after me, can you see them?" she said, looking back. They all picked up their ears, but there was only the sound of silence.

"Don't worry we are here, and there is no one after you," Ash said slowly, rising to the occasion.

"Perhaps we should go back." Menaka looked concerned as always.

"Yes, and meet leopard and friends, they are bolder in the dark." Rose wasn't convinced.

"What's your name?" Dylan asked.

"Usha," the girl replied. "I was kidnapped near the *Udawatte Kale*, on the way back home..."

"When, when?" Dylan got up with excitement, rudely interrupting her story.

"About a week ago."

Dylan slapped his knee. "I heard my mother talking about it, it was in the local newspaper. You are from Diyatalawa, and you disappeared near *Udawatte Kale* reserve while walking back from school right?"

"Oh! Yes, yes." Usha's eyes glowed. "Three men wearing masks suddenly came from the forest, and held something over my nose and... and..." She was about to break down again. "When I came around, I was in a room. I was there for a long time. That night they blindfolded me and took me in some vehicle for a long time. Then they took me out, tied my wrists tightly and carried me, taking turns. It was dark, freezing, we climbed and climbed for hours, and then came to this cave, close to here."

"Did they hurt you?" Menaka asked, eyes growing wide like saucers and fearing the worst.

"No, no, they gave me the best food, fried rice, Kottu roti, chocolate ice cream. One of them was very nice, h-he had a very gentle voice and said they will take me home soon, said they were friends, and some people were trying to hurt my family and they were only protecting me there." Usha was beginning to relax. "Then I asked why they had to cover their faces if they were friends? Then this man just stroked my cheeks and said nothing, he had very soft hands."

"But how did you escape?" Ash was curious.

A laboured hum came out of nowhere; it grew louder and more urgent.

"What is it?" Menaka asked with concern.

"Oh my God! It's Dylan," Ash shouted. "He's got the wheeze."

"Oh no! He's struggling. Please, we have to do something. I can't watch," Menaka said.

"He needs his puffer," said Ash.

Menaka released Sindhu and quickly laid Dylan's head gently on her lap. Rose clapped her palms over her ears; his audible struggle was too much. Usha and Sindhu watched helplessly, scared.

"Please Dylan breathe with me, please, you can do it, do it for me, please," Menaka crooned, rocking him a like a baby; her tears ran freely. "Please breathe, please."

She was pressing his head tightly against her chest. The hum stopped and the regular rise and fall resumed. Menaka was crying and smiling at the same time. Rose sighed. Ash looked at Menaka, his face glowing with respect.

"Th-thank you Menaka I am ok now," Dylan whispered feebly, and fell asleep on her lap.

"It's them!" Rose yelled out, and pointed. There was a sea of lights coming their way.

Rose started running, Ash groped blindly after her, still groggy with sleep and numbed by the cold. There was loud shouting as the torchlights gave chase. Rose screamed as she stumbled over another gravestone and came down hard, her ankle throbbing with pain. Ash turned back to rescue her. Dylan and Menaka didn't move; he had sensed the hopelessness and placed his arm tightly around Menaka. She stroked the Pirith Noola holy string around her wrist, blessed by Buddhist priests, fervently. Dylan recited the Lord's Prayer silently. Usha and Sindhu had vanished. Rose screamed as she was caught.

"Hey over here." A gruff voice crawled over their nerves. Soon chaos reigned as the others caught up with them.

"Sir! Sir! Over here, I think it's them." Ash leapt towards the voice – he recognised it immediately. It was his father's estate manager Ranjan's voice. Soon he was looking at his father's concerned face.

"You should have just told us where you were going at least, you idiot, you didn't mention Bakers Falls," Lionel spoke gently. There was much noise as everyone started talking all at once. Usha reappeared out of the mist. Sindhu too limped back.

"Lucky Thanga had spoken to that little kid Sindhu just before you left, he thought the kid knew his way around as well."

"Sorry father, we spent too much time at Bakers Falls and got caught in the storm." Ash took on the responsibility.

"Good, hope you at least took a dip in the rocky pools, you were too chicken to do it before,"

Lionel said in a hushed tone, full of understanding.

"And we saw a leopard!" Ash said with excitement.

"Wow! I have never seen one in this area, ever, and I have been here all my life. That itself might make this drama you put us through worthwhile," Lionel said calmly. "And did you take a photo?"

He was more excited.

"No, missed out." The disappointment bit in to him now.

"That's ok; you've had a rare experience."

He stroked Rose's head with affection. She smiled back at him, eyes brimming with affection and respect. Rose was with Muruga uncle, who was part of the search party. Her red pottu looked jaded, the rain had spoilt its sparkle.

"And who's that girl?" Lionel said, pointing at Usha.

"Oh! She's the girl from Diyatalawa who disappeared about a week ago."

"Oh my God, no way." Lionel's features changed quickly. "Where did you find her?"

His brow contracted to a concerned frown.

"She found us, poor thing was in shock and she was running away from some people, and the funniest part was we thought you were them and got a nice shock," Ash elaborated.

"Ranjan! This is the girl from Diyatalawa who disappeared, remember? Apparently she'd been kidnapped. Please get her some warm clothes and food, get them all some warm clothes and food, we'll have to report this to the police as a priority."

Dylan's heart sank when he saw his father in the search party, and he braced for the inevitable. His look said it all; disdain dripping over Dylan and Rose.

"This is the last time you are going after this stupid monster business, you hear me? Bloody waste of time instead of studying, look at the fuss you put me and Mummy through." Rex muttered his accusations in Dylan's ear.

Dylan knew he was just warming up; bigger and better stuff lay in wait to be enjoyed at home at their leisure – he didn't want to go back home.

"And you have rubbed mud over our family's name, look at the people here, half of them are common workers from Lionel uncle's estate, what won't they say when they see you have been with Rose at this time of the night?" Rex continued, still in a low voice. Rose was not the only member of the fairer sex in his group, Dylan wanted to point out.

"She is from a background that has no class, don't you have any shame?"

Dylan looked at his father with undisguised fury. Luckily Rose was out of earshot.

ONE TREE HILL

CHAPTER 5
CONSEQUENCES

The police sergeant was obviously displeased and took great pains to show it. He was thin and tall, with a sagging belly, a stupid looking moustache parted at the centre, teeth stained a bloody red by a lifetime of chewing betel leaves, and he burped quite frequently. He was half asleep and was looking at Usha with absolute loathing. 'I have better things to do at this hour than taking a statement from a stupid kidnap victim' seemed to be his quite overt message.

"So what's your age again?" he asked with his hundredth yawn.

"Nine." Usha was scared. She had already related the story of how she was drugged and taken to the cave.

"How many were there?"

"There were mostly three, the fourth one came occasionally. But sometimes I heard new people, voices outside the cave, they never came inside," Usha said.

"So could you recognise any of them?" he asked again when she had repeated that they all wore masks all the time.

"No, just their voices, the fourth one was very kind and gentle, the others called him boss," Usha said.

"Oh! Now we are getting somewhere, could you describe this man?" The Sergeant's interest had miraculously picked up.

"No, he looked younger than the other three, with a long-sleeved shirt and trousers and wore better boots than the others, and visited only twice, after the first day."

Usha struggled with her memory.

"See sir, I think this is just not good enough, first she says she never saw his face or their faces, and now she says he looked younger, no credibility in the story." The Sergeant was looking at Lionel.

"No, no I meant his body and voice appeared younger than the rest." Usha was close to tears.

"Sergeant do you also think that she bound her own wrists to give herself those RED CUTS?"

Lionel's voice made the policeman half get up. His authority and affluence in the town carried weight.

"Yes… sir, good point." The Sergeant was apologetic. "So, how did you escape?"

He was more respectful now.

"Today, after dinner…" Usha started.

"Yesterday you mean?" the Sergeant corrected with a forced smile. It was almost 1.40am.

"Oh sorry, yes yesterday after they gave me fried rice and chocolate ice cream, I heard a terrible sound, like… like a wailing sound or a scream and, and… it got louder and louder."

Usha finished half of her fifth glass of water in one gulp, sweat raining down her face.

"I covered my ears because it was so very loud, then I heard screams and shrieks as something attacked the people who were playing cards near the entrance by the fire as they always did, then… then…" Usha paused with fear. "Then I saw this giant animal, much, much bigger than any man, I am sure it was an animal, jumping over the fire. I… I screamed and ran to the back of the cave."

Usha stopped again.

"Must have been a leopard or a bear." The seargent was almost deferential, treating her with feigned kindness they all knew. But he was definitely interested.

"No, no, I have seen leopards on TV; this one was very, very big and standing. Then there was a long, long silence and I came out. There was food scattered everywhere and a big branch had fallen near the fireplace, and I ran and ran and met these nice people who helped me."

She pointed towards Ash, Dylan and the girls with a shy smile, referring to them as elder brothers and elder sisters.

"Ok, a giant beast was it?"

The sergeant looked at Lionel with a sarcastic smile. Lionel was clearly uncomfortable, struggling with the animal bit as well. Dylan, Ash, and Rose exchanged looks at the same time. They were bursting with excitement. Menaka looked despondent.

"Ok, we are almost done little girl," the seargent said with a highly condescending smile, straightening his back with a concluding air. "But what about this white garment you are wearing, did you always wear it?"

"No, they gave it to me just before dinner, I am sure they were preparing to take me somewhere, and... and it was an early dinner," Usha said.

"AND HOW do you know that?" The seargent raised his voice and lowered it in mid sentence.

"I heard the 'boss' man asking the others to take me to the place at least an hour early since there were landslides on some roads, he came this morning... sorry yesterday morning, that was the last time I saw him." His volume had scared Usha.

"Ok, we're done. Don't worry sir, we'll get the teams to find out more, leave it with me."

The seargent looked at Lionel with a wide smile, getting up.

"I have total confidence in you Seargent," Lionel smiled back with a look of absolutely no confidence. "And I will come back later today to meet your Inspector as well."

The seargent's face fell.

They emerged into the visitor area of the police station. They had brought home a kidnap victim, but they were made to feel like criminals by the seargent. A tired and exhausted looking couple leapt on Usha and began hugging her. Usha's mother stroked her from head to toe, like a statue, absorbing her return. They looked like a couple leading a modest, no frills existence.

"Daughter! We almost died with worry, we knew something bad had happened."

She was crying and smiling, her mouth trembling. As soon as they had finished their descent, Ranjan had phoned Usha's parents with the good news. Lionel had alerted Menaka's mother. Usha's mother gently kissed all four with love and gratitude, rubbing their cheeks affectionately with her palms.

"Thank you, thank you for bringing my daughter back safely." Her kind eyes were red with tears and grief. She suddenly held Menaka's hand and pointed excitedly at her wrist.

"Oh look! Daughter, you have a butterfly-shaped birthmark, just like my girl, look."

She pointed at Usha's cheek. They were identical and could not have been told apart. Usha's father nodded his head with gentle acknowledgement. He was a very thin man with grey hair and unkempt stubble.

Manel smiled gently. Dylan had his eyes on the ground. He could face his father, but not Menaka's mother. He just wanted to be her chaperone again, her guardian, he knew he had compromised his position. Manel aunty got up silently and left. Menaka followed her without a word or look. Dylan watched Menaka disappearing into the dark outside; he could still remember her fragrance in his mind, in his nostrils. He fought off a crazy impulse to run after her and kiss her, instead looking jealously at Thanga who was holding both Rose and Sindhu with simple relief, and at Ash who was walking out with Lionel uncle. With a sigh he submitted his immediate fate to his father, walking out into the pre-dawn darkness.

As expected, Dylan received his punishment, and he received it with minimal protest.

"But we saved that little girl didn't we?" He had wanted to save some face towards the end of the thirty-minute early morning ear bashing.

"What! Saved what, is that what we spend on you for, to save some mad kid in the mountains, I don't believe a word she said, some cock and bull story for sure." Rex Perera was tired and furious. "I AM TELLING YOU RIGHT NOW, drop that stupid project."

Dylan had retired with a smile. He was immune.

"Hello," Ash croaked, terribly sick and groggy with sleep.

"Hey, it's Dylan, get off your arse."

"What the hell, it's only just five past eleven, what's wrong you idiot, and it's Saturday, and I'm dying from a cold," Ash barked.

"Hey! Did you see those flower petals that were stuck on Usha's garment yesterday, those pink things?" Dylan totally ignored Ash's exhaustion.

"Yeah, I think so, so what?" Ash was lost.

"They're from the Pink Nelu flowers, they only bloom once a year and only in late March and April, peaking during the Sinhalese, Tamil New Year season, but we're in November now, SEE?" Dylan burst out in one breath.

"So what, you idiot?" Ash was getting impatient.

"That means they are in their off season. There must be a patch or field somewhere lying around, we find it, we find Usha's cave or its rough location, got it dumbo?"

Ash hung up on him.

Dylan was still excited. He couldn't wait. He walked straight over to Rose's house, he didn't care about his father's restrictions and he knew that he could look Thanga straight in the eye anyway.

"Master Dylan, Rose is still asleep," Thanga said, as expected without an atom of reproach. Dylan winced as always as that dreaded 'master' prefix came out. He had some print outs of the Pink Nelu flower in his hand.

"Don't worry I'll wake her up," Dylan said.

Meena was sweeping the front yard and greeted him with her usually maternal smile. Dylan banged on Rose's window. She opened it, still half dazed.

"Oh no! It's you, can't I sleep?" Rose complained.

But he soon had Rose hooked on his theory. Half an hour later they were heading towards Sindhu's house. Rose took the short cut that passed near Muruga uncle's farm. Dylan stopped to absorb the postcard view; the waterfall whose waters trickled over the dirt track and fell over the precipice right next to it, cloning itself, the natural seat made of rocks, and the emerald green pasture across it.

"How do you find these places?" Dylan asked Rose, his voice immersed in awe.

"Well I'm not a rich brat like you, spending the majority of my time indoors, you know?"

Dylan kicked some water at Rose.

"Hey! Nooo!" she squealed.

"You know that girl loves you, don't you? Please tell me that it's gone in to your thick skull?"

Rose said out of the blue. Dylan was silent, his pulse on fire.

"If you don't tell her now, you will regret it, and you don't deserve her."

"I know, you wait and see, I will ask her when I meet her next, I wouldn't be able to live with myself if not. I… you know how much I love her."

Rose looked at him and said nothing.

"Yes, I know where it is, this is the only place it grows this time of the year," Sindhu said with a casual air. The previous day's adventures had hardly left a mark, and the gash on his knee looked like it was healing already. Dylan slapped his back and almost knocked him down, passing him a bag of toffees. Sindhu's eyes lit up.

"As soon as the weather clears I will send you a message ok? Be ready on that day, we have no time to lose." Dylan couldn't contain his excitement.

"It might be better if we take Muruga uncle this time; he knows the area better than me," Sindhu said sheepishly. Dylan thought it was a capital idea. On the way back they brought over Muruga uncle; single-toothed, genial and old Muruga uncle in on the conspiracy.

"Sir, just come over here early in the morning on any day. I am always here before eight, then I take the herds to graze," he said.

"Hello?" Dylan was tired as he answered the phone.

"Hey, run that theory past me again." Ash had somehow unclogged his nostrils and throat of some of the infection. He sounded more like himself.

"Get lost, it might be too complicated for your mediocre grey cells." Dylan pretended to be unforgiving.

"Ok, ok I get it, if those flowers were an annual event around April but found now, then… then there should be an off season patch somewhere, right… right?"

"Yes, exactly, and Sindhu knows where it is and I'm heading there with him and Muruga uncle tomorrow morning," Dylan said with a superior yawn.

"Hey, don't you even think of going without me, ok see you tomorrow, smart arse."

Dylan was breathing hard and smiling as Ash hung up the phone.

It was a lesson in patience for him as Sunday and Monday were washed out, and torrential rains covered the town in mist. The Horton Plains and surrounding peaks were nowhere in sight, it appeared as if the heavens had claimed them for their own. The hourly quota for a day seemed to have exceeded twenty-four hours for Dylan. He had no hope for Tuesday either, as Monday night was taken over by a stubborn drizzle. He woke to a perfectly warm and brilliantly blue Tuesday morning, and rushed through the morning drill for school. He called Ash – it was a worthy cause to play truant for. He called Menaka's house nervously but when Manel aunty answered he hung up, too gutless to face her over the phone. They were in luck though, as Muruga and Sindhu were both available.

It was different to the route to World's End or Bakers Falls, a much steeper climb, and had to be approached from the mountain trail known as One Tree Hill. Even Sindhu was panting hard as they climbed up the mostly mossy and stony mountainside, treacherously wet from the recent torrents. Ash and Dylan had to unplug leeches that had wriggled in to their socks driven by blood lust. The salt-water treatment prescribed by Muruga uncle worked like a charm as they dropped off without a fight. They slipped regularly as they crawled slowly, looking more like soldiers on a battlefield than two amateur climbers. A spirited sun beat down on their backs, drenching their school uniforms with sweat.

They had left their bags at Muruga uncle's house, and had their jackets tied around their waists. It was hard to imagine the same landscape buttoned in by mist and cloud. Muruga uncle was shockingly the most agile out of the lot of them, an old cloth around his head and sarong folded in two, stepping over fern and stone on a pair of patched up rubber slippers with a casual whistle on his lips. Dylan was clearly terrified of heights and kept looking down obsessively, while Ash did not look down at all. Dylan was silent the whole way, totally unbothered by the flora and fauna around him or his usual pedantic need to elaborate on them. He missed Menaka.

They arrived at a large clearing, more like a small soccer field or park hewn on to the side of the mountain, and it was all pink. Soon they were wading through a sea of Pink Nelu; it was a hidden treasure tucked away in paradise. The field ended against another steep wall of the same mountain, rocky and dotted with trees at the base.

"Can you see any caves?" Ash was tired of scanning the surroundings.

"Come sir."

Muruga grabbed Ash by the arm and led him towards the rocky surface. Suddenly they could see a crevice hardly big enough for a baby to crawl through appear in the rocks. The crevice soon transformed into a massive entrance to a partly underground cave that was accessed through a series of broad steps. It was a brilliant natural optical illusion. A shudder ran down Dylan's back as he recalled Usha's story. The signs of a fireplace were clearly evident from the burnt marks, charred wood and ash stains on the ledge nearest to the entrance of the cave. Dylan was terribly excited with his own detective work.

"What did I tell you? Always trust me."

Dylan couldn't resist it. Ash was in awe and conveyed it in silence. The cave was freezing cold with very little light coming through. There was absolutely nothing inside except for a soggy King of Spades and Ace of Hearts from a pack of cards at the very back of the cave, swept by the winds, they suspected. They came out and Dylan looked closely at a massive branch that had fallen just outside the entrance. He grabbed Ashwin's camera and started snapping away, having forgotten to bring his camcorder in the mad scramble in the morning.

"What is it, what is it?" Ash was looking too, desperately trying to figure out Dylan's reaction. Dylan was pointing silently towards something on the branch, breathing heavily. He had gauged Ash's grudging respect. There were massive scrape marks on the wood that ran from three very deep incisions; they looked like giant claw marks. But it was the dark, semi dried sticky substance that was in the furrows that had excited Dylan the most.

"Could it be the Yakush?" he asked Muruga excitedly. Muruga uncle looked closely, with an air of experience.

"Looks a bit too big for a leopard sir… but…" He swallowed his words. Dylan knew that he was skeptical about the Yakush, but too respectful to say it.

"But how did Usha escape? If she had run straight down, she would have gone over the edge from where we came from this morning, you know?" Ash said with a shudder.

"Look sir." Muruga uncle pointed towards a small footpath that snaked in to the mountains right next to the cave. Ash gave a low whistle.

"Lucky girl, that was one hell of an escape."

They got back well before the finish of school at 2.30pm. They had left Muruga uncle and Sindhu happier than when they had started, with hefty tips. They had time to kill, so they made a beeline to the Nuwara Eliya grounds and joined some school kids who were playing soccer. Ash had no problems integrating. He threw an admiring glance at some attractive schoolgirls from Ladies College Nuwara Eliya on the road home; it was laced with his 'magnetic smile' as he had modestly labeled it. They did not return the favour.

"What happened to your special touch?" Dylan enjoyed the episode.

"They weren't worth a second look, I just wanted to add some colour to their boring existence," Ash commented with a pretend yawn. "At least mine will always be your track record multiplied by a zillion, right?"

Dylan struggled for a retort in vain.

Ash approached his house cautiously, although he knew he had no reason to. He found his mother in tears, his father on the phone. His heart sank.

"What's wrong?" he whispered to his mother, since his father was still on the phone.

"That girl Menaka left the house, leaving a note asking Manel aunty to forget her, that she won't be coming back, and Aunty doesn't know why." His mother fought through her tears.

"What, when?" Ash felt the ground spinning.

"This morning, she actually got on the school bus and had even got off at the school. Aunty Manel wants your father to get some help from his friends in the police, she does not want it going public. You know how rumours fly, and father is talking with his DIG friend in Colombo now."

"Hello?" Dylan sounded tired as he answered his mobile.

"How are you?" Ash's voice trembled.

"Duh… nothing major has happened since I last saw you forty minutes ago," Dylan laughed. Ash was silent, figuring out what to say next.

"Hello?"

"Yes I'm still here… obviously you haven't heard?" Ash took the plunge.

"Heard what?"

"Menaka has run away from home," Ash blurted out in one breath. There was a twenty-second silence.

"Hahahahaha, nice try, there's more than four months left until April 1st you fool," Dylan laughed loudly.

"No, no it's true, mother was in tears and father was contacting his friends in the police, aunty does not want any details going public." He could hear Dylan's breathing.

"What! Why? Manel aunty didn't give her a hard time over last Friday did she?" Dylan's voice was breaking. "Hey, this better not be a joke."

He was almost pleading.

"Does it even sound funny?"

Dylan hung up abruptly.

Dylan's mother was banging on the door.

"WHAT? What?" Dylan's anger was muffled by the pillow he was sobbing into.

"Did you know that Menaka has run away somewhere? Manel aunty just called." She waited for his response. But none came. "Who would have thought, I always thought she was a sweet and decent girl you know, you can't read anyone these days, perhaps she has run away with some boy. Looks more like it."

Dylan was glad the door was firmly locked from inside. He wasn't sure of himself, what he would have done if he went out. He turned back to his pillow.

"Father, I have to tell you something." Ash approached his father.

"Yeah?" Lionel said, distracted by the Daily News. The concern on his face, however, was for Menaka. He adored the girl.

"Father," Ash gulped.

Lionel finally put down his newspaper and gave Ash his undivided attention.

"We – me and Dylan – well he had a theory on where to find the cave that Usha was held in, and… and we took Muruga uncle and Sindhu and went there, this morning. AND we found it."

"So you cut school?" his father said.

"Yeah."

"And, can you pick up the notes from someone? You know that all these classes can add up to your Advanced Levels right?" Lionel asked.

"We covered most of this stuff in the tuition class at least two weeks ago," Ash replied.

Most of their subject teachers at school belonged to a rapidly growing club of entrepreneurs who made staggering margins from their mass tuition shops. They were shops where education was bought at a high price. They selflessly withheld critical topics at school so that the young savants in their care could receive a more rounded knowledge, in their own classes.

"Ok, look, are you sure it's the same cave?"

"No doubt at all." Ash had a good feeling, borrowing his confidence from Dylan.

"Ok, I will call the Inspector; you know they haven't found it yet?"

He got up with a tired smile, shaking his head.

"Ok, the Inspector is going to dispatch a team first thing tomorrow, and he is going to take Muruga. I will send a message to Muruga now," Lionel said ten minutes later, settling back into his chair. Ash was about to leave.

"Look son," Lionel said without looking at him and picking up his paper. Ash knew the tone.

"I hope you and Dylan haven't lost Manel aunty's trust with that episode last Friday, or was it Saturday? She never said a word against the two of you, but you let her down. It only takes an instant to lose trust, but to build it, much, much longer."

Ash received the wisdom in silence, and with some guilt.

THE TUTOR

CHAPTER 6
THE TUTOR

Dylan rang the doorbell nervously – Ash was with him. Priyantha opened the door, his blue eyes lighting up with recognition. He was drying his hair after a shower.

"Hi little brother, you're Menaka's friend right?" he asked with a kind smile, adopting the adult position of an elder brother. Dylan had not got over his shock.

"You're Priyantha right?" Ash spoke, smiling and warming to the guy's tone and smile.

"Yes, yes, how did you know, did Menaka tell you?"

"Yes," Ash replied. Dylan was still silent, now more with indignation than anything else.

He was struggling to hate the man, though.

"Aunty, Menaka's friends have come," he called Menaka's mother softly.

Dylan was nervous again. He was still struggling with his embarrassment from the previous Friday. It was Thursday and they had decided to visit Menaka's mother.

"Oh, come, come in." Manel aunty motioned them in without a smile, but it was not a look of anger, and the boys felt at ease. She looked like a ghost, sleepless eyes had retreated right back into their sockets, and she had lost weight almost overnight. She looked like the living dead. She motioned them to sit and promptly started crying. Dylan and Ash watched uncomfortably, then Ash sprang to his feet and embraced her. He was struggling with his tears. She clung on to him with affection. Dylan was still speechless and immovable. Priyantha had disappeared into the house.

"Look at what this girl did." Her voice trembled. "Did… do any one of you know if… if she had met someone… or… or was with someone?" she asked anxiously.

"No aunty, I am sure she wasn't with anyone." Dylan finally found his tongue.

Priyantha walked out dressed in smart pants and a long sleeved shirt, holding his helmet.

"I'll see you this evening aunty," he said softly, and worshipped her by touching her feet.

"May the Buddha bless you," she said from her heart.

With a shy 'See you' to the two boys he walked out. They heard him bringing out his bike from the side of the house.

"That boy has been like a son to me. He was visiting his parents in Kandy on Tuesday when I called him to tell him about her note, he rushed back the same day and asked me if he could stay with me and support me you know." Manel aunty's sore eyes lit up with affection. "He has so much to do for his engagement fixed for December, but he says he will manage it somehow. I would have gone crazy over the last two days if not for him."

The boys exchanged quick looks.

"I always paid him a little extra for the lessons because he was struggling, and got him more lessons with some of my friends, but he always treated me with respect and affection, like… like a mother." Manel aunty struggled with her tears again. "And he looks after Devon, with all his school work and his food; he might think I don't care for him anymore."

Menaka had left a vacuum that was hard to fill.

"Wow! So the guy is going to get engaged," Ash said, breaking the silence on the way home.

"Yes." Dylan was in deep thought. "He seems to be a nice guy."

"Yes he does, he looks cool."

The phone blasted the silence. It was 11.25pm and Manel aunty was about to take her sedative for the night. Priyantha promptly answered the phone.

"Hello?"

Silence.

"Hello?"

"I want to speak to mother... please, who is this?" Priyantha went white. It was Menaka.

"Where ARE you little sister, your mother is worried sick, where are you?" Priyantha asked in one breath, affection simmering in his tone.

"Sir, is that you? Is my mother ok? Please tell me." Menaka was crying. She had always called him sir in respect of their teacher-student relationship. He had asked her to call him elder brother, but her mother would hear none of it.

"Menaka, she is not eating or sleeping, WHY did you leave, what happened?" His tone came out unexpectedly strong.

"Who is it son?" Manel asked in a faint voice from her room.

"AUNTY! AUNTY! Come quick, it's Menaka," Priyantha shouted. She was by the phone in a flash.

"Why? Why did you do it? How could you do it to ME, how could you?" she accused her daughter, crying. Priyantha was looking worried.

"I am fine mother, I am ok, I will come to see you soon, I promise." Menaka was sobbing loudly.

"You know after your father left, how I looked after you, you KNOW THAT don't you? When you decide to come home I will be dead, I promise you that."

Manel was clutching her heart. Priyantha grabbed her hand with a yell. Devon luckily slept through the commotion; his exertions at school had knocked him out.

"Hello? Menaka, please come home..."

She knew Menaka had hung up. She sank to the floor in a faint.

Lionel and Ash came immediately – Priyantha had called them. Manel trusted Lionel and Florence more than her former neighbours, the Pereras.

"Please, I am fine now Lionel, this silly boy thought I had suffered a heart attack or something. I'll be fine, can go tomorrow." Manel did not want to bother Lionel and Ash.

"We are going anyway, so don't argue." Lionel was firm; there was no room for negotiation.

"You stay with little Devon, we will take aunty," Lionel said.

"Ok uncle," Priyantha had replied meekly, looking lost.

"No! No Lionel, no photos, just imagine the damage it will cause her reputation, who will marry her, if it got out, you know our people don't you, they will condemn her even if she was not with someone," Manel moaned from her hospital bed.

They had kept her for two nights for observation. An angina attack was the official verdict, and stress was deemed the main culprit. Lionel had again asked her permission to release a photo to the media for a public appeal, but she stubbornly refused to budge. He had mentioned the call to the police and they had traced it to an isolated public phone booth in Bandarawela. He knew the police had downgraded the priority, treating it as a teenaged love tangle.

"Don't you dare tell anyone about the police dropping the search, definitely not Manel aunty, Dylan and that Rex or Dorothy, ok?" Ash knew to obey when his father used that tone.

Dylan, Ash and Priyantha sat around her bed in silence. Anxiety still clouded Priyantha's handsome features.

"And, and after that call I know she is fine, that she is ok."

Her sigh reverberated in the room. Florence stroked Manel's head gently.

"You don't worry about anything on the home front ok? We are there, don't worry about ANYTHING," Ash's mother assured her. She had supplied Devon and Priyantha with a fridge full of food while Manel was away.

"Oh, thank you Florence, thank you so much, we have burdened you so much, you know Devon says he enjoyed your food more than mine," Manel said with a smile. Priyantha's face lit up as well.

"What nonsense, what are friends for? It is nothing." Florence's tone was enough to kill any doubt.

Ash, Dylan and Priyantha came out in to perfectly clear skies and sunshine, but it was typically fresh November weather. Rose was waiting outside.

"Priyantha, this is our prickly thorn, Rose." Dylan introduced Priyantha to Rose with a smile. Rose smiled rather shyly, totally out of character.

"Hello little sister." Priyantha shook her hand, addressing her with his usual kindness mellowed by age.

"What soft hands," Rose commented promptly, back in form.

They all laughed.

"And you do look like Hamid Khan," she said.

"And who is that?" Priyantha looked puzzled.

"Whaaaat, you haven't heard, that famous Bollywood actor, where were you?"

Priyantha laughed, Rose hid her blush beneath her dark skin.

"I don't have time for movies little Rose, and I don't like movies where they run around the flower bushes, changing clothes at least five times during a single song."

They all laughed. He was warming quickly towards her, just as quickly as she was turning starry-eyed with him.

"And I have an engagement to plan, you know. You will understand one day," Priyantha said. They were beginning to feel exceedingly like kids with him, and they didn't mind.

"Did, did Menaka know that you were going to get engaged?" Rose asked.

"Of course she did, she even joked that she wanted to be our bridesmaid one day. Why?"

"No, nothing," she said, sidestepping the question and looking at Dylan. Dylan knew, and did not acknowledge her glance.

"Do you have a photo of your girl?" Ash asked.

Priyantha whipped out his mobile and showed them a photo of a classy looking girl with short hair and super sexy figure, wearing shorts. Ash whistled softly.

"I'm sorry, but SHE is stunning."

"Thank you." Priyantha blushed. "She is studying in the States, doing her masters in law," he added.

"How did you meet her?"

"You'll never believe it – on Facebook and then it became serious when I met her when she came down for a holiday with her family."

He looked embarrassed.

"And does she have a name?" Rose pestered him. Priyantha laughed.

"Natalie Fonseka."

"Hey, let's go to our place, for a cup of tea," Rose suggested.

"Thanks, only for fifteen minutes though, ok? I have three music classes and an economics class today. Very busy on Saturday afternoons," Priyantha said.

"Come sir, come," Meena greeted Priyantha with a reverent smile.

"Come Master Ash, come Master Dylan," Thanga joined in. Dylan and Ash winced and looked with guilt at Priyantha. Rose was the least bothered.

"This is paradise Rose," Priyantha said, referring to the location and stroking little Raju's head affectionately.

"Thank you sir," Rose said automatically.

"Not YOU." He looked at her, with a reproachful look. Rose laughed. Meena served them plain tea with a piece of juggery, an exotic sweet prepared from palm tree extract.

"Mother, this is the best tea I have ever had," Priyantha said, addressing her with filial affection and taking a sip. Her eyes shone with tears and she hurriedly turned away to hide them.

"Sooo… did you and Menaka have something going?" Priyantha asked casually, looking at Dylan with a mischievous grin and biting on a piece of juggery. Dylan almost choked on his tea.

"HOW DID YOU KNOW?" Rose jumped in, giving Dylan away. Dylan was silent.

"Oh, I know these things. It was always Dylan did this or that, it became a nuisance just listening to your name. When a girl says these things you know," Priyantha said, still smiling.

"Yes, monumental crush, but this idiot never asked her out," Ash said.

"Why?" Priyantha asked.

"Because that's what this guy is, Mr. Procrastination and Mr. Pessimistic all in one." Ash looked furious.

"I hope she… she is happy somewhere, and now I am happy I didn't ask." Dylan finally spoke, his voice faltering. Priyantha leaned over and squeezed his shoulders hard.

"C'mon Dylan, you really think she is with some boy do you? Surely you must feel it here that she loves you, don't you?" he said, tapping Dylan's chest. "Above all we all know she is the sweet and reserved type – how could you ever think she ran off with some guy?"

Priyantha's logic rocked Dylan.

"Then where IS she and who with?" Dylan asked passionately.

"I really don't know, but my suspicion is she is held by force, I didn't even tell this to aunty, it is better for her to think that Menaka is safe somewhere," Priyantha said, a frown clouding his forehead.

"But… but she did write a note, and it was her handwriting, and… and Manel aunty was at home at the time, right?" Rose wasn't too sure.

"Yes, that's something I can't get my head around, but we will find her and she WILL marry you, ok? Keep that picture." Priyantha gave Dylan's shoulders another firm shake. Dylan was choking back his tears.

"Will you help their affair?" Rose asked with a naughty smile.

"Oh ho… no way, after they finish their degrees, yes, but NOT before, I respect Manel aunty too much."

"When will you bring him back? He is soooo nice," Rose whispered in Ash's ear when they were getting ready to leave.

"Hey Priyantha! Rose…"

Rose kicked him hard and Ash laughed. Priyantha left a five-hundred rupee note in Raju's hand as they left.

Dylan answered his mobile.

"Hey, I checked out Natalie, she is hot, hot, much hotter than those photos on his stupid mobile," Ash gushed.

"Who?"

"Natalie Fonseka you idiot, Priyantha's girlfriend," Ash said.

"Where did you see her?"

"On Facebook of course, she is very relaxed with her account controls." Ash was on Facebook. Dylan did not enjoy such graces.

"There are some photos of our joker on it as well – Priyantha," Ash laughed.

Dylan yawned.

"I don't know why I bother."

Ash banged down the phone.

The sound of crackers echoed through the mountains. December 1st had finally arrived. The churches rang their bells. It was the first official warning of Christmas. The mornings and nights were icy cold, but flawless blue skies ruled the heavens during the day. The radios suddenly started belting Frank Sinatra, Elvis Presley and Boney M nonstop. Dylan hated the sound and the music. He didn't want any celebrations. At one time, as recent as a month ago, he couldn't wait for the season to arrive. Menaka had not phoned again, and the police had openly forgotten the case. Manel's absolute determination not to go public had settled the matter as far as they were concerned.

Dylan wasn't too sure if Menaka's father knew, Aunty Manel had nothing to do with him anymore. And Priyantha had postponed his engagement indefinitely.

"How can I? Not when aunty is like this, she is like a ghost now, have you seen her recently?" he had said, his features drawn with worry. Dylan and Ash looked at him with admiration.

They had seen her.

"But is Natalie ok with it?" Rose asked.

"Yes she is fine, she respects my decisions, see I wear the pants," Priyantha had said with a weak smile.

"Are you sure about that?" Rose had laughed.

"What is wrong with Dylan, is he still worried about Menaka?" Ash's mother had asked him one day in the car after Sunday Mass. His father was driving.

"He... he," Ash sighed, "he had a huge crush on Menaka."

"But she just turned sixteen!" Florence sounded surprised.

"Oh come on Florence, how many times has your son been seen loafing with girls in shopping centres, damn pretty ones too," Ash's father said calmly, eyes on the road. Ash blushed and Florence looked at Lionel with disbelief.

"Anyway, you don't support any relationship between them, you understand? He is Catholic and she is a Buddhist, you know what Rex uncle and Dorothy aunty are like," she said.

"But, but, what has that got to do with anything? Did Lord Buddha or Jesus Christ teach us not to fall in love with a person from a different set of beliefs or faith?" Ash sounded indignant, totally out of character.

"That may be under normal circumstances, but Rex and Dorothy are NOT normal," Florence came right back at him.

"Yes true, that boy is damaged as it is just living with them; don't make matters worse for him and us," Lionel agreed with a sudden grin.

"I've got an idea, why don't you take him to Nalin uncle's place for Christmas? Get his mind off things. Nalin uncle was pestering us to come, but we might not have time, I've got some foreign buyers coming to sample some of our tea, we'll see," Lionel said. Nalin was his brother.

"That would be fantastic, will Nalin uncle and Darshani aunty mind?" Ash was breathing hard. He'd had some of his best Christmases with them.

"Of course not, you know they love having a crowd for Christmas, more the merrier for them," his mother said.

Dylan was mildly excited. His parents were overjoyed.

"Nalin uncle is on the Board of Commerce in the south, good business-man just like Lionel uncle, it runs in their blood," his father said, drawing on obvious social and economic parallels with their family. Dylan felt a strange sadness saying goodbye to Priyantha, although it was only for two weeks. He was both a parent and a brother, a classic hybrid between adult and teenager, gliding effortlessly between both dimensions.

"Enjoy the two weeks Dylan, get this out of your system at least for a couple of days, and remember, HOLD that picture of the two of you together, don't lose that ok?" he had said softly.

Manel aunty was a broken woman. It was clear that Devon missed his mother, even though she was near him.

"Enjoy yourselves, I will treat my daughter as dead and give a seven day alms to the Buddhist priests," she lied. She was referring to the tradi-tional Buddhist practice of offering clergy and friends a meal consisting of the dead person's favourite food on the seventh day after death. It was clear to both of them that a single smile from Menaka would send Manel aunty scrambling to greet her back to life.

HE RESTED ON THE REDEEMER'S HANDS

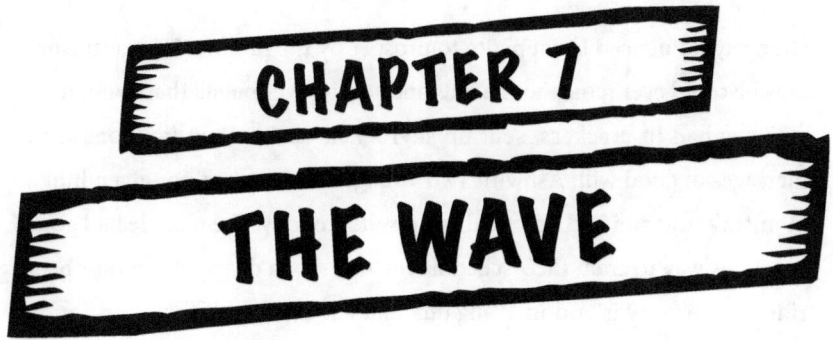

CHAPTER 7
THE WAVE

It was early morning and the sky was a perfect sheet of blue. They laughed as Ash executed the perfect dive on Dylan's kite. Dylan kicked sand in Ash's direction to prevent the kill. But too late, his kite descended elegantly onto the waves, destroyed.

"Hahaha, you think a rookie like you could beat me?"

Dylan was itching to have another go, just to shut Ash up. He couldn't remember the last time he had flown a kite. It was at Gall Face Green when he was just twelve, the hilly winds and the trees made it impossible over in Nuwara Eliya. The beach was packed with holidaymakers. The sound of crackers was still in the air. Christmas Eve had snuck in and snuck out the day before. The boys had already spent a glorious week at Ashwin's uncle's house in the coastal city of Matara. It was Dylan's first visit to Nalin uncle's house.

Their favourite monster and the project had faded back into myth, and with it dreams of the one million rupee award. They had no appetite for it any-more. Dylan was still wracked by intermittent bouts of desolation, anger and guilt – guilt for not confessing his love and anger for being a wuss. Priyantha had phoned them to say that Menaka had called again and she sounded much happier. The news had made Dylan feel relieved – she was safe.

They had been stuffed with southern culinary delights by Ash's aunt, who was a legendary cook. Crumbed prawns, curried prawns, pan-fried seer fish, sea crabs, Ambul Thiyal and batter-fried cuttlefish had corrupted Dylan's taste buds repeatedly. His depression, and their swims in the sea, had strangely influenced his appetite to prosper by the minute. He was unsure how he could ever return to the hills and survive without all that seafood.

They had lit crackers, sent up skyrockets and helium balloons with messages of good will. Ashwin's two younger cousins had not given him a moment's rest, and he'd had no time to sulk properly. Nalin uncle had gone out of his way to cram their schedule further, scuba diving and motor boat rides to a nearby island in Weligama had left the two of them pleasantly exhausted. Sleep had come uninvited after each hectic day. The airwaves around the house had been filled with carols, and the Christmas tree had to be decorated.

Dylan dreamt often of Menaka being with him to enjoy the fun. They had all celebrated midnight mass at the famous Matara cathedral on Christmas Eve, famous for its miracles. Dylan was in awe of the giant statue of the crucified Christ. He had sipped some King Coconut wine at the banquet on Christmas day.

Suddenly there was a collective gasp from the crowd. They were all pointing at the sea excitedly. Children were squealing with excitement and curiosity. Dylan looked. The shoreline had receded by a few kilometres; there were fish and prawns jumping on the now exposed seabed. The kids were running with buckets to catch them.

"Ash, hey look! This is crazy, look," Dylan yelled.

But Ash ignored him completely and was looking towards the road, transfixed on something. Dylan was about to push him when he saw what Ash was looking at. Menaka was standing calmly looking right through them. Dylan could not move, as he joined Ash as a statue. She was standing under the shade of some coconut palms by the main road with an old and hunched woman. Then Ash came out of his trance and started waving wildly, screaming "Menaka! Menaka!"

They tore towards her, ploughing through blurry faces and bodies. Knocking people down. One man threw a belated punch, but Ash ducked it easily. Just as they reached the road they saw her getting on to a bus with the old woman. Dylan raced to a Tuk-Tuk parked on the kerb and jumped in with Ash.

"Where to sir?" The man looked up, putting aside his newspaper, the hope of a hire shining on his face.

"Please… please go after that bus," Ash panted.

"Why? Look I don't want any trouble, I am an honest man."

"I will double your normal fare, I promise," Ash spat out. Dylan was silent.

"Then I will follow the bus around this island, if we have to," the man said with a broad smile, parking his hard won honesty briefly.

He yanked on the gearstick and turned the vehicle in one reckless burst, breaking all the speed limits as he cut and chopped through the traffic. There were horns, abuse, but the man was one with his machine, eyes intent, every bit a local James Bond. The sea breeze rocked the little machine as they sped through. The bus didn't stand a chance against their driver. They just wanted to overtake it and hop on at the next stop. Suddenly he stopped, got off the Tuk-Tuk and started to run like a mad man.

"Run! Run!" he screamed, pointing towards the sea. A blue and green ridge shimmered out in the distant horizon and it was getting bigger and moving like a rocket towards them.

"Wave! Wave! It's moving fast."

There was screaming, kids fell, got trampled, stood up and fell again. Parents flung themselves over them; people were jumping out of their vehicles, leaving them on the middle of the road.

Dylan started running blindly towards a bunch of tall coconut trees on the other side of the road. He heard his heart exploding in his ears, his lungs screamed for air, a cyclist slammed into him, but he felt no pain as he got up. He was almost at the trees when he looked back for Ash. It was a wall of water. He had no time to scream, even to feel fear. Suddenly it was dark.

"No! No! He's coming around, keep going, there, there."

Dull voices floated through. Dylan felt his lungs being crushed, scratchy lips smashing against his. Brilliant sunlight exploded out of nowhere. He gasped and covered his eyes, dazed, and coughed and coughed until the residual seawater left his lungs. Blurry images of a fat face, bearded, and crooked lips smiled at him. His chest throbbed with pain.

"You, ok?" The voice came out loud. The screams hit his eardrums again. His right eye was covered in water. He wiped it with the back of his hand, and saw it was a dark red. He could now feel the gash on his forehead. He touched it gently and winced. He felt himself shaking violently, and his legs wobbled as he got up. He was on a concrete island; cars, vans, floated around him, some had people in them, trapped, their screams painted on their faces. His concrete refuge was jam packed with people, and some lay on the floor.

He saw the fat bearded guy again, giving CPR to a young child. He saw the giant sign on a rooftop across the street, barely above water, *Palace of Fashion*. It was an island-wide clothing emporium. They had been there several times, him and Ash, with Darshani aunty and he had loved it to death. Then another bus floated close to them. Passengers were outside clutching, clawing at its windows, and he saw Menaka screaming and holding a window. The little boy right next to her let go, the current carrying him away.

"Please, please that's my sister, my only sister." His energy picked up as he screamed, pointing towards Menaka.

He knew 'girlfriend' would not have worked; sisters were more material. A dark young muscular guy next to him looked at him, then at Menaka, then jumped in. He swam, struggling against the current, stepping on vehicles, dodging animals and tree trunks. The crowd cheered him on. He finally reached Menaka, hooked her arm around his neck and swam back, his struggle now infinitely worse with her added weight. She slipped from his grip several times, but he was stubborn as hell. He finally reached them and lifted her over, his strength gone, smiling with relief. A sea of hands reached out for him, but as they did there was a surge of the waters, and an enormous tree collided with his head. He went under the raging torrent, so close to his rescuers; the crowd screamed. Dylan could have sworn that he sank with a smile on his face. They pulled Menaka up and gave her to him, limp with exhaustion.

Dylan didn't, couldn't say anything. He just held Menaka in a tight hug, stroking her head.

"I thought… I thought, I lost you for a second," he whispered into her ear.

"Get off you, you sicko!" she lashed out, and now he looked into dark eyes viciously lit with anger and disgust. Shock had numbed every muscle in his body. He thought she was going to slap him, and jumped away is if electrocuted. Some on the roof looked at him suspiciously, but their focus thankfully returned to the conquering sea.

"I'm sorry, I was just relieved that you were saved, I…" Dylan stammered, still reeling.

"Really? Well I'm grateful, but better not take it any further," she said, a shade softer this time, face still suspicious.

Dylan couldn't mobilise his body or his speech.

Dylan had been front of him one minute, and the next Ash was being torn apart by the water. He went with the flow and didn't fight the current, relaxing his muscles. Then there was a huge object in front of him, and jarring pain in his left shoulder as he smashed against it. He could see the light at the top; his lungs were about to give up. He clung to a twisted looking ladder on the side of the object and got on to the top, and the light, coughing and sucking in air desperately. The world was filled with the sun.

He was on a train engine; the name was carved at the top, *Ruhunu Kumari:* the Southern Express from Colombo. The current was dragging it fast; water swirled around the top. He could see passengers on another carriage slipping away as it toppled, screaming. He looked at the shattered landscape silently; he forgot everything, even the pain in his shoulder. He saw tourists stranded on the roof of the *Seasands Hotel.* They had tucked in to a wicked buffet there just two days before Christmas.

The current took his engine through the broken wall of a huge building. It was very familiar; he recognised the Matara cathedral, where they had ushered in the Christmas just two nights before. The huge statue of crucified Christ had only the outstretched hands remaining. He saw his chance and jumped onto the hands. The engine swept away. He thanked his maker and prayed silently, something he had not done in a long while. He sat on the Redeemer's hand and rested. He could see the pews with some devotees still stretched on them, looking back at him from their watery grave. He shuddered, and moaned in agony as his shoulder moved. It was late afternoon and the waters had stopped rising. He heard noises and a boat appeared, with two young guys dressed in shorts and black vests.

"Guys, guys," he shouted. They almost fell into the water.

"Please could you take me, my shoulder's broken," he begged. One of the men shot him a strange look, then smiled sarcastically.

"Piss off."

The men calmly dived into the water, and began relieving the bodies of their gold chains, watches and other valuables. The indignity and desecration tore into Ash's conscience.

"Help! Murder! Murder!" he screamed, rage pulsing through his body.

One of the men threw a piece of wood from a broken pew at him; he ducked it easily.

"Shut up, or we will kill you, you little brat," he shouted, his features mottled with hate.

"Murder! Murder!" Ash screamed on. He was getting in to stride, his lungs inflating to the occasion. Goading them to give up. Suddenly there were yells. Two more motorboats tore inside, filled with people.

"They're stealing from the bodies, stealing," Ash spluttered, his throat going hoarse at the critical moment. But it was enough – they heard him. The brutes half drowned as they were kicked and punched, some women joining in the fun as well. The Samaritans helped Ash down into one of the boats gently. He came out into a post apocalyptic world, trying to remember what it looked like before. The land was part of the sea, there was no beach; he wasn't sure where one stopped and the other started. Uprooted trees, broken houses, buildings, wrecked vehicles littered the landscape. He saw giant Monitor Lizards swooping in on easy prey, and black crows squabbling for their place at the feast. He saw the Red Cross boats. He was hauled into one. They passed more submerged rooftops, and then he saw Dylan and Menaka. They were being lowered in to a police launch.

"Dylan! Dylan! Menakaaaa!" he screamed silently, his voice gone.

"Hello?" Manel's voice quivered.

"Manel, Manel, this is Florence, thank God, Dylan and Ashwin are safe, Ashwin just called, his left shoulder has been broken." Florence fought with her tears, but quickly recovered. "And do you know WHAT? He saw Menaka with Dylan, I have no idea how she got there."

Florence was almost shouting.

"No, please… please can this be true?" Manel stammered.

"Priyantha has gone home for a couple of days because his mother is sick, are we leaving now? I will bring Devon as well, can we leave now? Please Florence." Manel's voice was pressing and desperate.

"We will pick you up in half an hour, Rex is coming as well," Florence assured her.

Manel stood unable to move as she saw her daughter, then swayed, her feet unsteady. Lionel jumped up and helped her to a nearby chair. They were at the Matara base hospital where most of the injured from the wave, the tsunami as it was called, had been taken. Ash saw Dylan next to Menaka. They acknowledged their mutual survival with a weak smile of relief.

"That's not Menaka," Manel said.

"What do you mean?" Florence almost yelled again.

THEY LOOKED AT EACH OTHER

CHAPTER 8

THE PAST

"We adopted Menaka when she was just one, Menaka and Neluka are twins, but… but we never told her… I couldn't," the ghost of Manel said, looking gratefully at Menaka's replica seated right next to her. Her eyes were dry. She had no more tears left to spill.

They were at Nalin's house, spared by the sea, an oasis in the middle of a desert full of debris, wreckage, the dead and the undead, who were weeping and searching for the dead or the missing. Nalin, Darshani, Rex and Neluka's uncle and aunty were outside on the verandah. Ash's two cousins kept peeking at the strangers.

"They were orphans; their parents had died in an accident. We didn't have any children for a long time, so finally we decided to adopt. We were visiting the royal ruins in Anuradhapura when our guide casually mentioned that there was an elderly couple struggling to bring up two babies – their grandchildren." Manel paused to catch her weak breath. "He took us there and we saw these adorable girls. I loved them both, but we could only take one. Menaka kept trailing me with her arms raised like a small puppy, we simply couldn't resist her charms."

Manel struggled with her voice. Yasantha shifted his feet uncomfortably. Jasmine was engrossed in her long exposed legs and high heels, surveying them with aesthetic self-absorption. She had no interest in the world outside, outside of herself. She was not the only one engaged in the adoration; Ash was providing plenty of moral support. His left shoulder was bandaged and his left arm in a plaster cast and a sling. She looked like Yasantha's daughter. Manel had eliminated her existence in the room, refusing all eye contact. Yasantha had found out that Menaka was missing only five hours ago when Manel wanted to announce her triumphant return. But that was not to be.

Dylan had his head squashed by a bandage, but he had escaped with only stitches. Seeing his father was yet another shock to him. Rex had wasted almost overnight, and he could see the pain of loss that had eaten in to him. He suddenly warmed towards his parents. Dylan was doing his absolute best to look away from Neluka, but he kept violating his resolution every half a minute. His gaze obsessively fell upon this stranger trapped in Menaka's body.

Neluka sat, staring stolidly in to the distance, right through them, and avoiding any contact with Dylan.

Florence and Lionel sat glued to Manel's side. Florence looked tired and had lost weight, which made her look a bit less roly-poly than usual. The shock of the tsunami and the boys getting caught up in it had smashed her world. Relief had only arrived when Ash had confirmed that both were ok. Devon kept looking at Neluka as if hypnotised, he simply couldn't get his head around the twin business.

"We lost touch with this twin from that day, until today." Manel aunty stroked her head fondly. Neluka released a weak smile, clearly uncomfortable with the open affection.

"I am so, so sorry darling, about your grandmother, must be so hard, hope they could at least find her body. Will give your family some closure. And... and to think that Menaka will never know her grandmother," Manel struggled.

"It's ok aunty, I was with her all my life, we were very close, perhaps that was all the ayusha, the life span predestined at birth, she brought with her. She must be at a better place now."

She spoke quietly, calmly, her words unburdened by emotion. Florence looked at her with shock and awe. Jasmine had her mouth open like a goldfish, Neluka's quiet resignation well beyond her intellectual grasp.

"Now I have another daughter, and I only hope that your aunty and uncle will let me borrow you for a few days during these holidays," Manel said with a glimmer of hope in her eyes. Neluka had been brought up by her maternal aunt and her husband, and they had moved to Matara where she had lived with her grandmother until the tsunami. She had lost her grandfather a few years ago.

Rose was in tears as she hugged Ash and Dylan. Ash winced as his shoulder hurt from her passionate embrace.

"Oh! Never thought I would miss you this much, I thought, I thought for a moment I would never see you again."

Meena went into a frenzy, dusting the chairs for them to sit down, crying and smiling with pure joy. She had dispatched Thanga to the estate shop to buy two bottles of cool drink.

"We didn't know what to do when Florence aunty came crying to see my mother on the 26th," Rose said. "We have been going to the Kovil twice a day and made several vows since then, you'd better come with me to honour those pledges," she said waving a warning finger. Promises made to the gods had to be fulfilled by those who made them, and the intended recipients of those blessings, in this case Dylan and Ash. If not there was fear that the blessings would revisit them as a curse.

Ash and Dylan said nothing. They just listened to her, grateful to see her again. Nothing was banal or routine anymore.

"And that idiot Priyantha switched off his mobile, I called him several times from a phone booth, he went home suddenly just before Christmas because his mother was sick," Rose went on. "I didn't know who else to call."

"We found a Menaka look-alike in Matara," Ash said suddenly. That was enough to shut Rose up.

"Meaning?"

"Menaka has a twin sister, and Menaka was adopted."

"What! You could never keep a straight face Ash," she said half laughing, part of her acknowledging that this was no joke.

"No, it is all true, Manel aunty told us herself, ask Dylan."

Ash motioned towards Dylan, who nodded his bandaged head slowly, with a disinterested look.

"The sisters are perfectly aligned in looks and perfectly non-aligned in nature," Dylan said casually, swatting at a fly.

"Well our boy here tried to play Romeo with her and what do you think…" Ash was about to share the episode, but stopped short when he saw Dylan's look.

"What do you mean? Will you stop talking in riddles?" Rose was curious.

"She's spending a few days with Manel aunty, you can meet her if you like," Dylan said quickly to change the subject.

"That'd be great." Rose was buzzing with excitement. "But… where is Menaka?"

Her face fell. It infected Dylan. They shared a silent moment. Thanga thankfully came to the rescue with the drinks.

"Drink Master Ash, drink Master Dylan," he said, filling their glasses to the brim. They were too exhausted to protest.

"And what about my glass, father?" said Rose, making a face. Thanga playfully squeezed her cheek.

Even Neluka had to concede a giggle as Rose gaped at her. Dylan sulked near the gate, self-conscious about his inelegant turban of bandages, while Ash adjusted his plaster cast with pride, his empty sleeve hanging loose by the side.

"Honestly I won't be able to tell the two of you apart, when Menaka comes back."

She was never ready to give up on Menaka.

"Oh… hey! I found something," Rose said and twisted Neluka's wrist with an apologetic smile.

"You don't have a butterfly-shaped birthmark." She looked like Archimedes as she beamed.

"And she always wears knee length skirts," she said, winking at Neluka's stingy skirt length.

"What do you mean?" Neluka said quite abruptly. Rose stepped back as if stung.

"I mean, just noting the differences, it looks so nice on you." Rose couldn't resist wiping her brow with a silent 'phew'.

Neluka stormed inside without a word.

"I think I would be able to tell them apart quite easily the moment one opens her mouth," Rose said to Dylan.

"I told you so." He mouthed the words with a broad smile.

"Now, that's going too far Rose, just because she is more serious, you have no right to rubbish her like this, she is more mature… and…" Ash couldn't keep it up as Rose gaped, taking the bait. He couldn't stop laughing.

"How could twins be so different?" Rose asked Dylan.

"I told you so," he mouthed again.

"Oh shut up, you and your 'I told you so.'"

Ash and Rose turned as Dylan expanded his lungs and held them.

Neluka came out dressed in a soft pink top and knee-length skirt splashed with equally humble pink, orange and yellow flowers. She walked out uncomfortably. They all knew she had worn it to satisfy a desperate mother's whim.

"We are going shopping, just the two of us." Manel aunty smiled broadly as they headed out of the gate. There was a barely perceptible spring in her step. The Tuk-Tuk she had organised sputtered to life and they disappeared in an angry cloud of smoke.

"Poor Manel aunty," Rose said, eyes misty.

"Yes, she is clinging on to every straw she can see, she has even stopped taking her sedatives," Ash said.

There was no pre New Year rush. The fervour and excitement had drowned in the December 26th tsunami. Neluka was about to cross the road to the Palace of Fashion, her hands full of clothes that Manel aunty had impulsively bought for her. She had said a firm 'No,' when she'd been about to buy a pricey purple top, and even Manel aunty had backed off. Then she saw the girl who had just looked out of the Tuk-Tuk on the other side of the road, trapped in a one-way traffic jam worming towards the town centre. Neluka dropped her bags and kept looking at the girl. The girl saw her. She got out of the Tuk-Tuk and kept looking at her. Lost in their own reflections, nothing else existed. Neluka knew who it was. Both couldn't move.

Menaka looked out nervously and saw her double across the road. The other girl saw her too; she was dressed in identical clothes to her. She saw the other girl drop her shopping bags in a trance. Menaka got out. Suddenly she saw Priyantha rushing towards the girl excitedly. Menaka screamed, recognising him, but the horns snuffed out the volume. A white van braked right next to her, with a screeching assault on the tyres, and a bearded man hustled her in. The girl screamed and kicked violently, passersby froze; the traffic cop saw it and got on with his job lazily. The van took off – Priyantha ran back and hopped onto his bike, racing after the van, his helmet still in one hand. The frozen people sprang into action. The mist was taking over now.

"They took a girl by force, kidnapped, did you take the rego numbers?"

A determined jumble of voices, and a fierce knot of people, milling around the same spot and galvanized into inaction. The cop finally decided to do something about it and headed towards the crime scene in slow motion. Then she saw her mother rush out, clutching her chest.

"Mother, MOTHER," Menaka's voice soared freely, above everything.

Nothing else existed. Her mother heard it, loud and clear. Suddenly her legs wobbled and she was about to fall. The crowd jumped and propped her up. Menaka sank into her mother's arms. They clung to each other, desperately, passionately. And the mist took over.

GOODBYE

CHAPTER 9

THE VANISHED

"How dare you accuse me?" Manel raised her voice unexpectedly. She was on the phone. It was 5.35am and Menaka couldn't sleep.

"You LEFT us! You have no right to ever judge me."

Menaka opened her door softly, and tiptoed towards the hall to hear more.

"She was with Dylan, I trust that boy, and she DIDN'T LIE, she just didn't say she was going to Bakers Fall, that's all."

Menaka's heart sank. Her mother was obviously speaking with her father.

"And there was this awful storm on the plains that day, you wouldn't know living in Colombo would you?" Her mother was sarcastic; she simply couldn't help it when talking with her father.

"And," she lowered her voice looking around anxiously, Menaka quickly ducked out of sight.

"And… you know I love her more than anything in the world, you have even accused me of favouring her over Devon… our… our own flesh."

Menaka felt the floor rushing to meet her, the walls, the dim light, they all spun around her in a wild orbit. She collapsed onto her knees softly and sobbed into her palms, her body rocking violently from the impact of suppressed emotion. She struggled back to her room and allowed her pillows to soak up the screams and tears.

Suddenly she hated her parents, her room, her house; she was a stranger and she wanted out. Her life was a lie; sixteen years of memories suddenly began to torture her mind and her conscience. She wanted to undo them.

The thought that she never could frustrated and isolated her even more. She had a sudden impulse to confront her mother, but didn't want to see her face.

"Don't be like your sister, that's all, you hear me?" Manel had told Devon while crushing him in a hug, just three days after they returned from the police station. Menaka's crime – lying about going to Bakers Falls and getting stuck on the plains.

"Menaka, are you ready? It's almost seven and breakfast is ready, hurry up or you might miss the school bus," her mother called out as she always did.

Menaka didn't reply. She was ready and had penned a painfully long note of eleven words.

I won't be back, don't look for me, just forget me.

She was not in the mood to offer any explanations; she wanted to inflict maximum pain. Guilt never entered her system, her heart had simply flipped. She came down, defiantly. Her usual stringhoppers, dhal curry, fish curry and pol sambol were spread out on the table; she could never survive without them. But her appetite was dead. Her mother was in the washroom. She found herself automatically dialing Dylan's number.

'This service is currently unavailable.'

The recording infuriated her, so she quickly dialed Ash. And it was the same. She wanted to smash the phone. She rushed back to her room, and took a long look. Her long row of dolls and the giant teddy bear sitting neatly on her bedhead looked back at her, they were alive, even mocking, challenging her to erase the history behind each one of them. She leapt onto her bed and dashed them in all directions, unable to take their disgusting gaze. She wanted to know who her natural parents were and why they had abandoned her. Menaka felt worthless. Her chest hurt like hell as she struggled again to hold back the flood. She took a deep breath and ran outside, forgetting her school bag. She absorbed their little front yard, her breath coming in fits and starts. The camellias, lilies, upcountry roses, mocked her. She had planted them with her mother, and each held a memory that she wanted to forget. But the more she tried the more they tore their way into her mind, her heart. She was weeping openly as she rushed to the school bus.

"Hey are you ok?" her classmate from Ladies College Nuwara Eliya asked with concern on the bus.

"No, no just a nasty migraine," Menaka stammered.

They got off at the school. Menaka avoided the knot of girls and parents going in, and quickly walked towards the main bus stand, near the quaint colonial post office.

"Hakgala gardens, hakgala gardens."

The tenth private bus to the famous botanical gardens slowed down, the conductor shouting the destination from the open stairwell of the bus. She got in absent-mindedly, and the bus took off without stopping. They were on a deadly race; the first to reach the next bus stand got the commuters and the extra revenue. It was business, and often commuters and pedestrians paid with their lives.

The bus skirted gorgeous Lake Gregory; the tourists already out on the boat rides, and the ponies for the kiddies' rides slowly being marched out. Part of the lake was still lost in the clouds. She had spent many outings here with her parents and Devon; she looked away. The cool early morning mountain air rushed through the open windows. She leaned forward and rested her head on the seat in front. The sweet bliss of sleep followed naturally.

"Tickets, Tickets." The conductor's voice grated through the darkness.

She got up and looked for her bag. Her purse was in it and the sweat appeared. The man was inching slowly towards her, wiping his mouth with the back of his hand.

"I… I forgot, sorry, I forgot to bring my coins," a little boy seated in front of her stammered. The man grabbed him by the collar and hauled him to the door.

"Hey!" he shouted to the driver, "stop the bus, this punk has no money."

He booted the little boy out in the middle of nowhere. Menaka saw him looking lost and crying.

She knew what to expect.

"Sorry, I… I left my bag at home," she stammered.

"Miss," he started respectfully, "that's what they all say, 'forgot my purse', 'I am sorry', this and that, but we are running a business, you should have got off at the next stop if you realised that you didn't have money, so don't talk bullshit."

His tone tore into her nerves, and she was trembling like a leaf, struggling for air.

"So, we are going to hand you over to the police, ok?" he said sadistically, relishing her fear, almost thriving on it.

"Please… please, I will give you my address…." she started, embarrassment now overtaking her fear.

"You think we have time for that, hey! Make a stop at the police station will you?" he told the driver gleefully. She could see the driver smiling back through the rear mirror, displaying his rotting teeth. They looked like the sort that enjoyed life's simple pleasures – bullying their victims to a slow psychological death.

"HEY stop that! I will pay her ticket."

A young woman sprang from behind her, and Menaka's heart stopped. The conductor's face fell. He was only just beginning to enjoy this drama. Menaka recognised the woman immediately. She was young. Menaka had seen her and her executive looking husband when they came to drop their son at the boys' primary school near her college. She had seen them for several weeks; they always smiled sweetly at her. She had smiled back effortlessly, recognising their decency. Both of them looked like models and the little boy was no different. She wondered what such a classy woman was doing on a public bus, she should have been in an expensive car, but she was overjoyed by the socio-economic inconsistency.

"Don't you have any shame, bullying innocent people when you see them?"

The woman was on fire; her little boy was still with her. The conductor collected her money and quickly retreated to the back.

"Don't worry, I am here ok?" the woman said, hustling Menaka out at the next bus stand, still glaring at the conductor and the driver. The bus resumed the race while they were still on the door well. The woman had her hair in a cute top bun, had long and pretty eyelashes, wore light lipstick and very little make up, and had a figure to kill for. The little boy looked at them, without a care in the world.

"Hi, I'm Sandra. Why aren't you at school today? Oh god, you've been crying, what's your name?" Sandra fired away.

Menaka finally broke down, she was comfortable enough. She couldn't talk; the woman quickly collected her to her chest, and looked around as several vehicles slowed down to take in the drama.

"Lucky I was on the bus, ok… give me your address, I am going to drop you at home."

Sandra didn't bother to find out her name. Menaka shook her head as if to protest.

"No arguments, luckily this guy developed a nasty cough just near the school gate, he does this sometimes, he soooo loves school," she said, winking at Menaka and tapping her son lightly on the head.

The boy suddenly collapsed into a coughing fit, remembering to stay in character. Menaka smiled weakly. Sandra took out her mobile and retreated to the trees to talk unhindered by the noise. She came back with a broad smile.

"We're in luck, there's this Tuk-Tuk guy I always trust, he is in the area and will be here shortly, my husband never allows me to travel with anyone else."

"But Sandra, please, I am troubling you." Menaka found her tongue.

"Didn't I say no arguments?" Sandra had finality in her tone.

The Tuk-Tuk came within fifteen minutes. The little boy held out his hand, giggling as the mountain air slammed against it, forgetting his cough again. Shame now possessed Menaka. She simply couldn't face her mother, and suddenly the fact that she was adopted didn't matter. She didn't want to know, she just wanted to embrace the woman who had selflessly guarded her all her life. Menaka felt that Karma had dealt her an instant blow on the very first occasion she had chosen to breach that trust. She saw the name-board of the protected national reserve *Seetha Eliya*, flash by. The driver suddenly turned into the reserve, through a dirt trail.

"What's wrong? Why are we stopping here?" Sandra asked.

"Madam, the engine's sounding funny," the driver said, suddenly hopping out, putting his glasses on and heading to the back of the Tuk-Tuk to check. Sandra let out a rude sigh and muttered 'just our rotten luck,' loud enough for the driver to hear. The man mumbled a stifled apology.

A white van suddenly stopped behind them in a cloud of dust. Two men hopped out and a rough tangle of hands yanked Menaka out of the Tuk-Tuk. They wore masks. She was numb, it happened so fast. Another man opened the doors of the van, also wearing a mask.

"Sandra, Sandra please, nooo," she screamed, but there was no one around. Her heart exploded in her ears, she thought she was going to die. But Sandra did not move.

"I need the final payment in my account by five, tell your boss, you understand?" Sandra said casually. One of the masked men nodded quietly.

"You really gave us a hard time the past few weeks, we simply couldn't get you alone, you should be a bit more adventurous like today, girl," she said with a mock yawn, smiling sweetly, then got back into the Tuk-Tuk with the boy.

Menaka felt all her muscles wasting away, and she resigned to it. The two men threw her onto the back seat like a rag doll, and forced her down flat on the seat. The van sped off, rocking and lurching along the dirt trail.

"Don't you dream of doing anything silly, I *will* kill you," one of them said.

She couldn't even if she'd wanted to. She knew they had hit a main road, as the sound of horns took over and the ride became smoother. Soon they re-entered the bumps and the shakes. The real and the unreal played a sick game of tag with her mind; she wanted to wake up. The van door grated open, and they tied thick cloth over her dazed eyes. She was too weak to protest and had no sense of time. They hauled her to her feet.

"Nimal, open the door, we brought the bird."

One of them banged on a door, laughing, his voice throaty. Menaka heard the bold chatter of birds and langur monkeys everywhere. She felt absolutely cut off and helpless.

"Wait, wait you idiots, who's going to see? And don't say my bloody name," a man inside said, opening the door, and his voice was familiar but she couldn't place it.

"Hmm, took a while, at least we can take a break now," Nimal, the familiar voice seeking anonymity said. She didn't even struggle to remember.

"And she is soooo nice isn't she?"

The throaty voice said. She could feel his lust dripping all over her. Revulsion ran down her spine in a slow crawl.

"Hey! Hey! None of that now, the goods must be untouched, uncontaminated, we have specific instructions," another voice said, a touch gently, but with clear regret.

They guided her over some stairs and put her in a room, then one of them removed the blindfold and they locked the door. The darkness restored her bearings quickly. The windows looked locked, shafts of daylight filtered through the cracks with ease. There was a bed with thick covers with some pillows in the middle, a desk and a chair, a clay water pitcher stood on the desk with a glass. A cupboard hid in the shadows. She quickly checked her watch; it was just 12.35pm.

She opened the cupboard. There was a pair of jeans, a thick jumper, and a woolen long sleeved top. She noticed a side door and guessed it might be the toilet. She heard the van leave, and suddenly remembered she was still in her school uniform. Her energy and confidence seeped back under the cover of privacy and darkness. She could hear her captors laughing outside. Suddenly the door opened and a tall, thin man in a mask came in. Menaka almost fainted with terror. He placed a covered plate on the desk, took a long, hard look at her, his breathing laboured and urgent, and left without a word. She guessed he was the sleaze bag. The meal was rich biryani rice, with roasted chicken, mint sambol and egg, but she had no appetite and she hated oily food.

She went to the windows and tested them, but they were barred from outside. She wondered what her mother was doing; she knew she would be tearing her hair out with worry. Menaka wanted to turn back the clock and reverse each action she had taken, but reality did not allow the fantasy to fester. She knew her mother would have raised the alarm by now, there would be people looking for her. The thought offered an atom of comfort. She thought of Dylan, Ash and Rose and the Yakush, their pet project from a life time ago. The tears came hard and strong – she missed Dylan. They all heard her cry. It was soon dark. She heard a vehicle approach, perhaps the same one, excited voices rising and falling, then the vehicle left. A different man wearing a mask brought her dinner and noticed that her lunch was still intact.

"Hey! Don't let me see the dinner plate still full when I come in the morning, they will not pay us if you starve to death, ok?"

Menaka recognised the voice that had mentioned about the goods needing to be uncontaminated. The guy who had talked down the sleaze bag, even if against his will. His voice carried tangible menace. She had to eat.

"Please, please tell me why you brought me here, my mother is sick, she will die if I don't go back, please," she pleaded.

He looked at her and left without a word. There were stringhoppers, seer fish and pol sambol. The meal brought back searing memories of home, but she was hungry. It was freezing and she crawled under the covers still in her school uniform, sleeping like a log until late afternoon. Her breakfast was on the table. Fried eggs with sausages, and she hated the oil, but ate out of fear. She dragged the chair to the windows and stood on it to look through the grille. The house was on a mountainside, higher up. She could see the morning mist still hanging over the landscape, dispersing fast under the sun. It revealed swathes and swathes of green as it lifted, and in the distance the glimmer of a large lake, with a cluster of buildings. Menaka knew she was looking at Lake Gregory and the chalets next to it. She heard gunshots;

soldiers from the nearby army cantonment were doing target practice. The proximity to friends and home left a promising glow. She wore the clothes from the cupboard, and the perfect fit intrigued her.

The vehicle had returned, it was Thursday night and very late. She checked her watch; 10.50pm. The door flung open, and the blindfold was back on in a flash. The men still wore masks.

"Please, please don't kill me, please, my mother will pay you anything you want," she begged. She could feel the end near.

"Please little sister, don't worry, we are just going to make a call that's all," said another guy, a voice she had not heard before, possibly the third guy from the van. He had the kindest tone of them all. Nimal was not heard again; perhaps he had left.

"Please tell me why I am here, please, my mother will be worried sick and she is not well."

She took advantage of his gentle tone.

"Good girls don't go to Hakgala gardens alone do they?" he said. They pushed her flat on a seat again. She guessed it was the same van. They bumped along, coming to a main road. It was freezing cold. The van stopped suddenly and they pulled her out. She began chanting pirith Buddhist prayers in a high-pitched tone.

"I told you not to worry, didn't I?" the kind-voiced guy reassured her with a chuckle.

She took a deep breath to rally her shredded nerves. She had given up on her heart, and she expected it to put a stop to her misery soon. A phone receiver was suddenly pressed against her ear.

"Now, we are at a phone booth, and you are going to speak to your mother and tell her that you are ok and not to look for you, that you are happy, ok? If you so much as hint that you are held by force, I will not be able to protect you from anyone here, you understand?"

"Ok," she whispered back. She told him the number.

"Hello?"

It was a man's voice and very familiar.

"Hello?"

"I want to speak to mother please, who is this?"

There was a second's silence on the other end.

"Where ARE you little sister? Your mother is worried sick, where are you?" the familiar male voice said.

"Sir, is that you, is my mother ok? Please tell me." Menaka choked on her tears recognising Priyantha's voice.

"Menaka, she is not eating or sleeping. WHY did you leave, what happened?"

His tone came out loud and angry.

"AUNTY! AUNTY! Come quick, it's Menaka," she heard Priyantha calling.

"Why, why did you do it, how could you do it to ME, how could you?" Her mother bore down on her conscience.

"I am fine mother, I am ok, I will come to see you soon, I promise," Menaka struggled.

"You know after your father left, how I looked after you, you KNOW that don't you? When you decide to come home I will be dead, I promise you that." She could hear Manel's breathing getting uneven. Priyantha's shout was still ringing in her ears when one of the men replaced the phone.

"That was good, see I told you there was nothing to worry about didn't I?"

She started breathing normally as she entered her cell again. Her mother dominated her conscience she knew something had happened.

The van left and there was a strange silence in the house. It was Monday. She knew that some or all of the three guys had left. Menaka had developed some resistance to the fear. The lake and the buildings taunted her daily through the grille whenever the mist allowed.

Her heart froze as the door flung open. The tall thin pervert stood at the doorway, his breathing louder than ever. He impulsively jumped forward, grabbed her, lifted her on his shoulder with ease and stepped out. Menaka began to struggle, she could feel his breath and it reeked of alcohol. She hated drunkards and even avoided walking on roads with pubs;

she was scared of them. He was acting alone; the house was empty. He took the stairs, keeping his balance. She continued to kick, her muscles turning against her again.

"Please, please, don't hurt me," she begged, her screams sounding impotent in the wilderness.

"Don't worry, I'm not going to hurt you, please don't struggle."

The voice bit in to her spine – it was Nimal. He leapt outside; the sudden flash of daylight dazed her, impairing her sight for a few seconds. She could see tall trees everywhere; he turned into the trees, Menaka still flung over his shoulder. The hairpin, still lodged in her hair from the last time she'd been home, flashed through her mind. She fumbled with it, but it came off easily. Her adrenalin stabbed it into his neck with enough strength.

"You!" He screamed in pain and half dropped her.

She made a grab at his head and the mask came off, and she saw fleeting images of a thin hungry face, moustache parted in the middle and red teeth clenched in pain. It was the police sergeant. The hairpin was still in his neck and the wound was bleeding generously. Menaka fell to the ground hard, but she didn't feel any pain. He was trying to pull the pin out; she was on fire and saw the rocks within easy reach. He pulled out the pin with a scream and pulled her by her feet, fist in the air ready to come down. The rock smashed above his ear. He went down with a yelp.

Branches whipped her face and arms as she ran and slid down the slope. Her jeans were ripped and blood flowed from the gashes, but the shock propelled her on. It was a beautiful, clear day; the mist had vanished without a trace. She felt exposed and cursed the brilliant weather.

"Come back, I promise I won't hurt you, I'm sorry," Nimal's voice panted after her. His voice was strained and growing faint. That charged her energy even more.

"Argh!"

A furry thing with huge curved tusks, followed by two smaller versions, charged out of nowhere, and her fear lifted her over them. She crashed on all fours, knocking her forehead. The wild boar did not turn back. It squealed with aggression and Nimal tore at his lungs in pain. Branches, boulders, moss, roots and more branches slashed her, ripping into her flesh with ease. Nothing bothered her.

She could hear the guns from the army cantonment getting louder. The thick vegetation suddenly gave way to a giant eucalyptus and pine reserve. Her tired legs sensed the ease and picked up speed. She could see a tarred road below, and she looked across and gasped. The lake had appeared out of nowhere, looking more its normal size. She looked back; no sign of Nimal. She scrambled on to the road with a huge sigh, but it was untouched by any sign of life. Menaka saw that the road wound around and below, down to the lake. She started running, her lungs suddenly caving in, as if sensing that the end was near. She saw the rip in her right shoe, her toes bleeding and bruised jutting out. One corner of the lake loomed in sight, a lonely tourist boat put-putted in the middle. Then she heard the sound of a motor-bike behind her. It skidded to a halt right next to her. She froze.

"Menaka, Menaka, is it you?" Priyantha's voice lapped over her depleted senses. She collapsed in to his arms with a painful sigh.

"It's ok, it's ok we're going home, but we must call the police first," he said, his voice trembling.

"Sir, I thought I'd never see you again." Menaka had no tears left.

"Shhh. Don't talk.'

He was still hugging her; she didn't want him to let her go. The tourists on the boat started waving at them, clapping. He helped her onto the bike with a gentle, 'hold me tightly,' slinging her arm firmly across his chest, steering the bike with his right hand. She wore the helmet. He rode slowly, the way he had come. Menaka swayed weakly, held only by his grip. The white van screamed in from the opposite direction and braked, blocking them.

"It's them, it's them, please turn back," she stammered in sheer exhaustion.

The side door of the van slid open and Nimal got out with another man. Nimal looked demented, his neck, the side of his head and thigh richly sprayed in blood. The other man was bald, a deep scar ran across his forehead like a trench and it still looked raw. Priyantha calmly dismounted and without a word pushed her straight into their arms.

"You bloody idiots, she almost got away, is this what I bloody pay you for?"

His blue eyes were clotted with rage, his handsome face disfigured, his tone unrecognisable. Menaka was too shocked to say anything. The van door closed and Priyantha casually remounted his bike and followed the van. Menaka watched him through the window, still struggling to weather the shock. Nimal suddenly sprang and gripped her throat.

"I will kill you! You bitch," he said under his breath. Menaka gasped for air.

"Hey! Get off; remember the boss is behind us."

Baldy, the man with the kind tone pushed him violently away. Nimal glowered at them both; it was only a matter of time.

"Why sir, what is this, why?"

Menaka was trying to look right into his glistening blue eyes, but he kept moving her target; they were back at the house. He was applying surgical spirits to her face and arms, gentle as ever. His features had returned to something of the normal face she knew. She saw that he was struggling with his shame, and perhaps pity for her. He didn't say anything.

"What did you do to my mother? I know something happened last Thursday, please tell me," she said. He looked up with surprise.

"You think I would do anything to her? She is fine, spent a couple of days in hospital, your call made her happy."

"Are you capable of anything? She treated you like a son, didn't she? And I looked on you like a brother, it's money isn't it?" Menaka shouted, rage contorting her face. He pushed the first aid kit aside and got up, impatiently. Guilt rode over him.

"And now I know that you kidnapped Usha, right? I never dreamt when she said that one of her captors had soft hands and a kind voice... Why her? She is from a much poorer family than us, why steal from her?" she shouted after him again, with reckless daring.

He went to the door and came back, looking straight at her.

"It's this bloody system," he said. She could only look puzzled. "Graduates like me have to scavenge for money, we ARE the majority, while the spoilt minority like you and your two friends who play with their PS3s and buy expensive vehicles like toys, you exploit the rest of us. I have no money even to marry, DO YOU UNDERSTAND THAT?"

Hate exploded from his eyes again. She was struggling to recognise the gentle soul with gifted fingers who taught her the piano for more than two months.

"So am I personally to blame for that?" She recovered her wits in a hurry.

"No." The words leapt out automatically, the simplicity of the question throwing him off guard.

"Isn't it more honourable to beg on the streets than this?" she said. He raised his hand to slap her. Menaka didn't flinch. The baldhead rushed up to check on the noise, along with the police sergeant. They had no masks on; she had blown their cover. Menaka immediately measured the risk, they couldn't let her leave or… or live.

"Make sure that not a single hair on her body is touched, you understand?" Priyantha said, putting his arm around the bald man but looking straight at Nimal. The police sergeant looked down sheepishly. Priyantha left and silence reigned.

Menaka applied medication to her cuts and bruises; her denims were in ruins. She checked the cupboard. There were three tops and skirts, the tops in different shades of pink and pinkish orange, while the skirts had simple pastoral floral patterns. She didn't have to take them out to know that they were her own, and she knew only too well how they got there. There was a thick white parka and two woolen jumpers underneath them. She sniffed her clothes, and felt her breathing growing shallow. She missed Dylan again, she just wanted one chance to put him out of his misery, tell him first. She needed that more than anything. Her living conditions improved slightly after Priyantha's visit, and she received a portable TV in her room.

Crackers echoed through the mountains and the mists as the 1st of December swung by. Priyantha had not returned and Menaka was getting fed up with her anxiety. She wasn't too sure which was worse, the stress or the impatient wait. Asanga was the most affable; the bald man with the trench across his forehead. The other guy, Sunimal, was the one who had threatened her over the food. He had a patch over his left eye, which still looked quite sore around the edges. Ugly craters pockmarked the parts of his face that weren't covered by his ugly beard, and he didn't know how to smile. She was terrified of him and wished he still had his mask on.

She wasn't sure if the names they used were their real ones. They took turns with her meals. Nimal was heard rarely, not seen, but she suspected he came in occasionally. Asanga had started calling her 'Miss' after the episode with Priyantha, and she picked up a look of genuine admiration.

"Please, please tell me why Priyantha is keeping me here for this long, please. You said you had a little sister of your own, around my age – think of her and tell me," she pleaded with Asanga when he brought her lunch.

Mentioning his sister brought instant dividends. He stopped in his tracks and looked at her with a spark of compassion.

"Ok, I will tell you, but Priyantha boss will kill me if he finds out that I have told you. Please, you don't know him, he has connections to the underworld."

"You mean people like you?" Menaka was bold enough to indulge her sarcasm, and was relieved when he smiled.

"Please, you should know me by now, that's not in my nature."

She gave him her most vulnerable look. He closed the door.

"It's for a treasure," he whispered.

"What!" Menaka almost shouted, then waved her hand in a silent apology. "What do you mean?"

She was lost.

"Well, there is this priceless treasure, apparently buried by an ancient king, in some rock vault or cave under a forest hermitage somewhere on the plains, just before he went into a crucial battle..." He looked around apprehensively. "The king's chief oracles used a powerful and binding mantra on two hot-looking virgins who had butterfly-shaped birthmarks on them. They were then tricked into entering the vault, and it was sealed with them inside. The belief was that the treasure would be forever bonded with the king even in the afterlife."

Asanga paused again and licked his lips. Menaka shivered.

"Well to cut a long story short, a virgin with a butterfly-shaped birthmark must be sacrificed at an auspicious time of year or month to find the entrance to the vault."

Asanga rushed through the last bit. Menaka couldn't talk; fear in its purest form had entered her mind.

"And now, Priyantha boss has found the exact location of this hermitage, they just want the virgin with the…"

He saw Menaka turning a bad white, blood draining from her face. He quickly gave her a glass of water.

"Please Miss, they might change their minds."

"And do you believe in this superstitious rubbish as well?" she asked.

"Not at all."

"Then why, why are you supporting Priyan…"

"I have to feed and educate three kids," he replied even before the question had left her lips. And the question was not that simple anymore.

"But… but how did you know that Usha had the birthmark?"

"Her mother had told most of the other devotees at her local temple, it is normally considered a lucky omen, so the word spread, and soon everyone knew, and our police sergeant heard it," Asanga said. "And you! I think was a fluke, Priyantha boss said he saw it by accident, didn't mention how, he hired that woman Sandra and another guy to tail you over several weeks, but you were never alone."

Asanga looked baffled. Menaka knew exactly how, her mother's kindness and Usha's escape had sealed her fate.

"Please, please, listen to me, my father is very rich and connected; he will look after you and your family, if you help me to escape. I will never betray you to the cops. I PROMISE," she said, tapping her chest.

"Nothing doing, I give you an inch and you want a kilometre," Asanga said, but he didn't look or sound angry at all, and his brow carried a calculating look.

"Wait, what happened with that scar across your face, it still looks raw doesn't it?" Menaka asked as he was turning away. He turned back excitedly.

"You won't believe it! That day, the day Usha escaped from her cave, we were playing cards outside when this, this, I don't know, animal, attacked us." Sweat trickled down his face.

"I… I tell you it was no leopard. Have you… have you heard about the Yakush? I am sure that's what it was, it swatted me like a fly and injured Sunimal's eye."

His face was drenched, but he went on.

"And the sound it made, you have no idea, it was inhuman. Luckily there were two others with us who carried us down and rushed us to a hospital in Haputale. Everyone believed us when we said it was a leopard."

Menaka had no doubt now. She smiled wryly as she recalled how once, the Yakush and the million rupees had dominated her life, their lives, less than a month ago.

"We told Priyantha boss, no more caves in the plains."

Asanga closed the door with a smile.

She saw it first on the TV, and heard the men shouting downstairs. The tsunami had struck, 40,000 had perished. She forgot her own plight for a moment.

"Miss, they are going to take you away today, this evening, it was decided suddenly, I don't know why," Asanga said in a rush as he brought in her lunch. He was perspiring heavily. It was the 30th of December.

"I will help you ok? I will not allow them to hurt you, but you must trust me, you cannot panic, that will give me away as well, you understand?"

Menaka gulped and nodded. It was well past 4pm when she heard a vehicle screech to a halt outside. She heard excited conversations below, and her nerves crawled all over her. The door flung open and Asanga and Sunimal stormed in.

"Quick Miss, let's go, there is no time to waste," Asanga shouted, with a slight wink.

The one-eyed Sunimal didn't say a word, just looked more intense than normal and twice as terrifying. It was the same white van, and they didn't force her in, but she lay flat on the seat just the same. The driver turned the vehicle with a vicious spin, and she recognised the police sergeant from the rear mirror. The van sped down the mountain, very close to the slopes, but Nimal and the van were one. Asanga leaned on her gently. She closed her eyes as the van tossed and rocked on the treacherous track. Suddenly Nimal stood on the brakes, and the van stopped. Asanga prevented Menaka's fall from the seat. The two men at the back followed Menaka's lead and stretched themselves over the seats as well. She heard two vehicles cross them.

"It's the police!" Nimal whispered. She got up and started screaming.

"Help! Help! Save me."

She caught a fleeting glimpse of tall eucalyptus trees, the tarred road through the trees, a police jeep taking the bend on its way up. The lake soared through the trees, filled with people. Then she was yanked down violently, and she gazed in to Asanga's furious face.

"You try that again and… and…" He stopped mid sentence.

She sank in fear; his face had lost its former promise, and she felt utterly helpless again. The van took it slow on the tarred road, held up by the evening rush hour she guessed from the orchestra of horns. Suddenly Nimal braked hard, and the van shuddered and skidded forward as the vehicle behind them slammed in to it.

"You idiot…" Sunimal started.

"Please one of you guys get out and take my place as the driver, if they recognise me, this whole show will be over, they all know me." The police sergeant leapt out of the driver's seat.

"Ok, keep an eye on her."

Asanga passed him a pistol openly, glaring at Menaka. She glared back, her trust in humanity abused yet again. Sunimal got down too. They closed the side door and locked it.

"What were you doing, idiots, braking in the middle like that."

She heard a riled male voice behind her..

"Hey SHUT UP! Or I will break your face; you should have kept your distance."

Asanga the bald thug talked him down. She closed her eyes with revulsion as Nimal the pervert and got comfortable next to her.

"Get out and RUN," Nimal whispered in her ear.

She opened her eyes. He was unlocking the side door.

"Get out you idiot, and keep running, this is your chance," he whispered, more urgently. She could see he was serious. Her legs wobbled, her muscles trying to tie her down again. She took a deep breath.

"Go!"

She leapt out and willed her heart and her legs forward, freedom so close that it had a toxic effect. She raced forward along a long line of vehicles, and heard a faint burst of voices behind her. She ran and ran, not looking back. Some people shouted at her, "Hey! You ok?"

But she never looked back, and finally she found the comfortable feeling of safety. She stepped in to a Tuk-Tuk caught in the traffic; luckily it was empty. She was panting hard.

"Please take me to No 176, Pussellawa Road."

She wanted to go to Uncle Lionel's house. The driver didn't ask any questions, happy with the hire.

Suddenly she was looking at herself, across the road. Menaka got out in a trance, unable to move – she didn't know who it was. She saw Priyantha racing towards the other girl, and screamed to warn her. Then she saw the white van brake next to her clone, its rear fender badly dented. Sunimal pulled her in. She saw Asanga bent behind the wheel. The mist swirled around her.

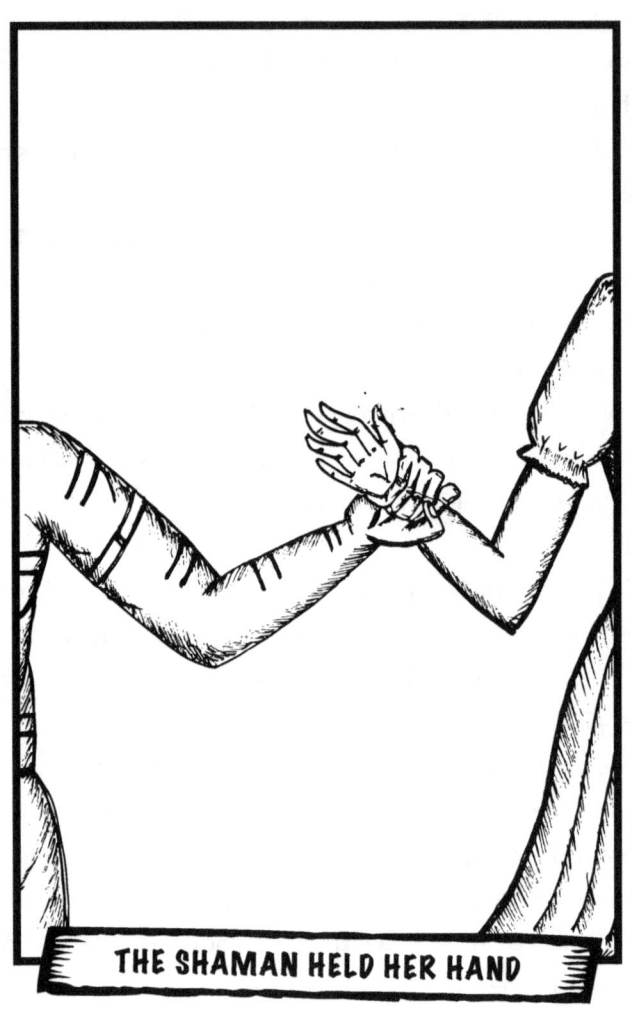

THE SHAMAN HELD HER HAND

CHAPTER 10

THE RESTORED

"I could strangle that animal; honestly I could, biting the hand that fed it." Manel was breathing hard.

Menaka squeezed her hand gently with an embarrassed smile; her mother had her arm hooked around her in an interminable squeeze. She had struggled to wriggle out subtly, but had given up when she saw that her mother had no such aspirations. Manel couldn't take it; betrayal and guilt had consumed her gentle soul.

"To think I invited that greedy snake into my house and offered it one of my two eyes," she said, looking desperately at Menaka. There were no tears, she had shed them all. Menaka shook her head in total disagreement.

"No, no don't be so silly Manel, how were you to know, even we wanted to adopt him as a son, he looked so kind and… and gentle," said Florence, quick to dissolve the guilt.

Ash made a face at her, sleeve still empty. Lionel looked at Manel, disapproving the comment. Devon was playing on Ash's PS3. They were in Florence's tasteful living area sipping sweet Nelli drinks. DIG Lucien Fernandez sat quietly in his immaculate khaki uniform, short graying hair and clean-shaven, his long career written on his carriage. Dylan sat silently, swimming in Menaka's eyes, his bandage turban forgotten. She invited him wordlessly, looking straight back, diverting her attention only out of politeness. His parents sat silently, gaping, looking slightly out of place as they always did when the De Alwis were around.

"No, no Manel, you are a great mother. We all know that, no?" Dorothy said, prodding Rex with an exasperated glance. He nodded his head vigorously taking her cue. Rex had even smiled with Rose who now sat in the background, trying to blend in silently but dying to speak with Menaka.

"But, but what about poor Neluka, can we, can we find her soon? Her aunt and uncle placed their trust in me, they will never forgive me. I am too scared to tell them."

Manel went pale again, the fate of her daughter's double weighing on her with ferocity.

"Don't worry, nothing's going to happen to her, we have a man inside their ring, you know our police sergeant?" Lucien said in his deep voice. They nodded, except for Dorothy and Florence who hadn't been at the police station that night. "Well the King of Spades and the Ace of Hearts that our two detectives found in that cave where the other kid was held were very useful."

He winked at Dylan and Ash.

"We found some fingerprints on them, we matched them against our central criminal database, but nothing came up. Then on a hunch we matched them against a separate database that contains exclusive internal staff records taken at the time of recruitment. And guess what, they were Nimal's," Lucien said with a sigh. "He was caught with his pants down. He broke down and confessed to Usha's case, but never mentioned Priyantha as the leader of the ring or Menaka's story. He said they had more kidnappings planned and that he could help bust the ring. He has four kids and pleaded for leniency."

Lucien took a sip from his drink; his audience couldn't wait for more.

"So we cut a deal with him three weeks ago – assistance to bring down the group for a shorter prison term. He had to go back inside and play informant and give us the heads up right in time for the bust. He readily agreed, and just this afternoon, he called our team about a house with a captive, and gave us the address. I think he got wind that the auspicious time for the sacrifice was imminent and didn't want to take a risk. But it must have got out, because we missed you by this much," Lucien said, bringing his thumb and index finger together.

"I… I think he caused that accident deliberately to help me," Menaka said softly. Dylan greedily lapped up her voice.

"Yes probably, but we haven't heard from him today," Lucien said, getting up.

"Don't worry Mrs. Fernando, we have the van's rego, and we will drill his parents and contact his overseas fiancee if we have to, don't you worry. The advantage we have is he doesn't know we are on to him. Ok?"

"Oh! Thank you, thank you, she just got over one ordeal, she cannot suffer again," Manel said, referring to the near miss with the tsunami.

The DIG went out with Lionel.

"Well, I'm glad you are staying with us until this is over, we'll have some good company for a change," said Florence, smiling mischievous at her son. Dylan's heart sank as his parents got up, it was well past 8pm; his parents emulated their former colonial masters by dining on time.

"If you want to hang around a bit, that's fine, but don't be too late." Rex threw him a lifeline with a yawn.

Rose winked at Dylan. Rex smiled again with Rose as they left, but Rose was too stunned to smile back. Dylan wasn't complaining, he blamed it on the tsunami. Manel finally released her daughter and went into one of the guest rooms flanked by Florence and Ash. There was a sudden awkward silence; Dylan and Menaka did their best to avoid each other's eyes. Even Rose struggled to find the right words.

"We missed you," Rose said after a forty-second silence, and flopped down next to Menaka. Menaka put her arm around her and collected her with a grateful smile, and without a word. Dylan nodded his head.

"How could you, how could you trust people in this world?" Menaka said, voice trembling.

"Shhh, it's over, and you came back in one piece, others are not that lucky." Rose applied the positive.

"Hey Prof! We should immediately call for another watch on the tree house, and resume our search for our monster," Rose said, suffering from a light bulb moment and scavenging for some normalcy. "And you know, Dylan has got some interesting photos of a branch with some holes in it."

Rose struggled hard to contain her explosive laugh, conscious that Neluka was still missing. Menaka did not take the carrot.

"I know now that the real monsters are with us, not in the jungle."

Rose went quiet.

"We should still meet in the tree house, as soon as your police guard is withdrawn and that bastard is caught," Dylan said with venom. He knew that there were several cops posted in the misty-white world outside; inside Ash's garden and outside.

"I can't believe that a woman with a little boy, maybe her own son, helped kidnap me. I mean how low could you get? And she was a pretty thing, could have easily passed as a model."

Rose shook her head.

"Why....why did you leave?" Rose asked, nervously searching Menaka's face. There was no hint of offence.

"I... My world caved in when I overheard my mother saying I was adopted, well not in so many words. I don't know what came over me, I can't describe what I felt. She was arguing with my father over our little trek to Bakers Falls."

"But why didn't you call one of us? I don't have a phone, I mean Dylan or Ash. We wouldn't have let you go," Rose said.

"These idiots had their phones switched off, that was the first thing I tried, their phones are as useless as them," Menaka said with a lively smile.

Rose looked at Dylan with mock reproach.

"But... but that can't be... Oh wait a minute, we were at Usha's cave or on our way there, our phones must have been off limits. Damn! Can't stop calling it Usha's cave."

Menaka shook her head with another sweet smile. The phone rang. Ash looked out.

"Hey! Summons from headquarters, you have violated your parole terms, you'd better waffle home leetle baby."

Dylan's sigh made Menaka laugh out loud; he had to burn more than nine hours to stage a comeback. It felt like a slow death. He wanted to be her guardian again, turn into a long distance lover, his resolve dissolving again.

"Ok, see you guys, I'll see you in the morning. Hope you get some rest," he said with a shy smile, and a lightning glance at Menaka.

"Hey! What about our rest?" Rose said.

"You sleep ninety percent of the day, so I hope you get to stay up for a change," Dylan replied, losing himself in a bit of their familiar stupidity. He shivered as he entered the clouds and switched on his torch.

"Hey!"

It was almost a whisper, and he turned around uncertainly. Menaka quickly planted a kiss full on his lips.

"I love you."

The mist took her back. Dylan stood still for a full minute, unable to move, not wanting to. His ears burnt and his limbs went liquid. He wasn't sure if it was fact or fiction, a trick of his preoccupied mind that was already fully occupied by her. He half turned towards the house and stopped again, then went home in a daze, the question still hurting him, entertaining him. He was on fire as he collapsed into bed, with no hope of sleep.

"Let me go you dogs, who are you? Let me go! Help!"

Neluka kicked and bit the hand of the bearded man who had dragged her in. He screamed and slapped her viciously across the face, his one eye conveying his sadistic bent. She was dazed for a second; too dazed to be sufficiently terrified by him. A bald-headed man was driving, and the mist was making it difficult for him. Her desperation increased as she saw the tall thin man, bound and gagged and stretched out on one of the seats, his temple a bleeding mess.

"Let's get the boss in," the bald-headed man said suddenly, stopping the van and looking back. The bearded, pockmarked one raised his hand again and Neluka ceased her struggle, briefly. The van stopped and a man on a motorbike braked next to it – the driver had turned the van in to a side lane.

"Who are you? Please let me go, please."

Neluka started kicking again. She caught a fleeting glimpse of the man who got in, hair swept back, chiseled cheeks and blue eyes mottled with rage. He slammed the door shut and held the chloroform soaked handkerchief over her face.

"Hi."

Menaka opened the door with a huge smile. Dylan stood, nerves braced, his facial muscles contracted.

"What's wrong? Looks like you haven't slept at all." Menaka couldn't remove her smile and Dylan couldn't restore his.

"Yes, not a lot," Dylan said quietly. "And you?"

"I slept like a log. It was a bit too cold though wasn't it?"

"Yes a bit," Dylan said, his heart stuffing his mouth.

"You look like someone who's been kissed by a ghost," she said with a wink. Dylan was ready to hit the ground, but he rallied and quickly leaned forward. Menaka didn't move.

"Hey, you're early." Ash popped out and Dylan pulled back with a silent curse. Menaka blushed, and went inside with a cheeky smile.

"Hey, let's go to town."

"What for?" Dylan was fuming.

"Oops, someone is in a bad mood, just to get some stuff for Manel aunty."

"Ok." Dylan quickly conceded his consent. He was burning again.

"Hey! Hey! Wait a sec, I've seen that chick before." Ash gave a whistle.

"Who?" Dylan asked.

"See, see the one who is, see there, crossing over to the Harpico store."

Ash was pointing openly; they were crossing the road to the supermarket. It still didn't feel like the 31st of December. The crowds were still poor;

they were still in mourning. Bodies from the tsunami were still being recovered. It was a brilliantly blue start to the day, and exceptionally warm. The girl stood out – killer body, short hair, long legs housed in a short skirt and nerve-wracking heels. She possessed sultry features and didn't look nervous at all on those heels as she walked smartly.

"Who is she?"

"Damn! Damn it's at the tip of my memory."

"Yeah right."

Dylan was skeptical. Ash gave up. Dylan missed Neluka; pity and guilt haunted him. She had been minding her own business in Matara, and he had somehow gotten her into this. He couldn't shake it off, but he had helped save her, that was the sole redeeming factor.

"What's wrong?" Dylan asked, noticing that Ash was sporting a stupid look on his face. People laughed at him as he walked through the shopping aisles like a zombie. Dylan knew he was squeezing his memory.

"*Natalie Fonseka.*" He slapped his thigh in excitement.

"Who?"

"Natalie you idiot, Priyantha's girl friend," Ash shouted. Dylan winced with embarrassment as people looked.

"Are you sure?"

"Of course I am, you think I would forget that face or figure?" Ash wanted to sound offended. His refined memory was questioned here.

"Let's go and talk then." Dylan turned towards the Harpico super store.

"Wait a minute, there's something funny here. I checked her FB page yesterday, you know because of Priyantha's business and all that; her last update made yesterday was that she was in Canada visiting a sick relative. So what's the story?" Ash stopped in his tracks. "Let's call Lucien uncle."

"Good Idea."

Neluka was still on a seat in the van when she came round. It was pitch black. The light inside was on. The man who was stretched on the seat had vanished. She was dizzy, groggy and struggled to get her bearings. The back door of the van suddenly flung open. Neluka looked up weakly at an exceptionally attractive young face with short hair. She shivered as the bitter night winds smashed in, but the fresh weather brought her faculties back fast. She was terrified.

"Please, please they kidnapped me, please… who are you?" Neluka gripped the woman's arm. She winced in pain, but gave her a warm smile.

"Please darling, don't worry, you are safe, you will be home in no time, ok? Trust me." Her voice carried authority. "I am from the Criminal Investigations Department, we followed your van and cut them off just in time, these guys are treasure hunters, and they were going to sacrifice you for treasure."

She sat down and propped Neluka on her shoulder with maternal concern. Neluka finally broke down.

"There see, it's all over, ok? No one can hurt you now, we got the driver, but the others escaped into the forest. We will take you to the hospital first, check you out and then home. I am Natalie."

"I am…" Neluka started.

"I know who you are darling," Natalie said with a reassuring smile. "Hey David shall we go?"

A young man with a police haircut, clean-shaven intense features, and military posture hopped into the driver's seat with a 'Yes Madam.' Natalie slammed the side door shut and the van took off with a jerk.

"David, please put the heater on, it's freezing in here," Natalie ordered the driver.

They drove for several hours in a world of black and white, the mist pressing against the windows. Neluka slept on Natalie's shoulder, utterly spent, the heat inside swaddling her like a velvet blanket.

Neluka woke with a start; she was on a comfortable bed. The sun was streaming in, and nature was making an unusually big racket outside. She suddenly remembered, and fear gripped her again. She was in a large room and on a king sized bed, but it didn't feel like a hospital bed. She checked her watch; it was almost 4.40pm. She couldn't believe it, she had slept a full part of a day. She ran to the door, and opened it into a large lounge area. Natalie was seated, sipping a hot coffee. She smiled when she saw Neluka.

"Why are we still here?"

"Relax darling."

Neluka hated the darling bit.

"Apparently the ring leader Priyantha is still at large, he has a reputation as something of a maniac and psycho, and might come after your family. We are under a police guard here, so perfectly safe. Here have some food, you slept like a log, which is good."

"Thanks but I am not hungry."

"Eat something please, you're probably still feeling nauseous, the after effects of the chloroform. At least let me make you a hot chocolate; don't say no, I don't want to take home a starved kid ok?"

She poured the hot chocolate. Neluka felt good after drinking it.

"The lunatics these days, you can never read them, this guy Priyantha looks so handsome, like a film star, and so… normal, very decent, I have been on this case for a while." Natalie had a glazed look.

"Blue eyes?" Neluka asked, her own eyes lighting up with sudden interest.

"YES, how do you know?"

"He is the guy who drugged me with the cloth in the van," Neluka said with a huge yawn. Natalie got up and went in to another room.

"I want to call my aunty please."

"What was that darling?" Natalie called from her room.

Neluka heard a phone ring just then. Natalie rushed out, flushing with excitement and a palm upraised for a high five. Neluka extended her palm half-heartedly.

"They got him, got him, let's go home," she said. Neluka sighed.

David hopped back behind the wheel and they drove for a couple of hours. It was night again, and a perfectly clear one. The moon and stars peeked romantically through the peaks. Neluka slept through it all, again. She was still sleeping long after the vehicle had stopped. She woke up and stared right into blue eyes set against a handsome backdrop. She screamed, willing her lungs, but her body was still weak and lifeless. Her head weighed a ton.

"Natalie, Natalie…"

"You can scream all you want now, no one will hear you darling. We are in the middle of nowhere." Natalie looked over Priyantha's shoulder, smiling sweetly.

"You witch!"

"Yes that I am," Natalie said, still smiling.

Priyantha looked at Natalie in adoration, as if worshipping a living statue. She turned with a snort, looking condescendingly at him. They were in a clearing, high up in the mountains and totally immersed in the jungle. Bats did low passes outside, an owl released a timely call, fraught with sorrow. There was a knot of people busy around an altar made of plantain trunks and tender coconut leaves, and a mountain of fruits; mangoes, pineapples, pomegranates, bananas, even betel leaves and rice on the altar. An old man with a genial face and a torso covered in white stripes was giving instructions. The exorcist was shivering in the cold. Neluka had seen them before, several times, and had even been to a devil dance and a Bali Thovil dance. The exorcist would go into a frenzy after communing with the gods or the demons, dancing and spinning, and would then fall to the ground. They would scream and shriek as they reached the pinnacle of their demented ecstasy. She had been terrified.

Her nerves crumbled as she realised why he was there. She was the sacrificial lamb, the carrion for the demons. She saw the *Maha Sona* devil mask or the *Ves Muhuna* on the ground next to the altar. Two lonely sky rockets streaked through the air in the distance – the New Year was only a few hours away. She felt like she was on a different planet, in a different world, a world that would end soon, for her. She froze as the Shaman came towards her with Sunimal and two other men. She knew screaming was useless, so she tried to focus on the rise and fall of her breath. She wanted to cram in a few seconds of *Aana Paana Suthra* meditation, face her departure with dignity.

"Come daughter," the Shaman said as he extended his hands. She held them out with a strange sense of peace. Then he panicked.

"Where is the birthmark?" he yelled, twisting her right wrist like a piece of clay. His geniality was awash in desperation and rage.

"What do you mean birthmark?" Natalie jumped in, not looking pretty anymore. Her voice was grating.

"See! Where is it? Didn't you say it was on her right wrist?" The exorcist twisted Neluka's wrist again. She felt the pain, but glared back calmly.

"I haven't seen, Priyantha has, I could kill that idiot, PRIYANTHA!" she screamed, like a woman possessed by an evil spirit. Neluka couldn't look at her face.

Priyantha rushed from the altar, avoiding Natalie's eyes, visibly shaken. The bald-headed driver with the vicious cut across his forehead threw his boss an amused look, evidently impressed by his weakness.

"But… but Menaka had it on her wrist, I… I have seen it so many times."

"I am not Menaka you nut, I am her twin sister, Neluka. I am from Matara," Neluka spat back with a sarcastic smile, her fear gone.

"What? That's bullshit, where is it damn it!" Priyantha presented a pistol against her temple. "What did you do with it? I will shoot you here like a dog, you don't know me."

The shots exploded in their ears. Priyantha screamed and fell. Natalie turned to stone, unable to move.

"Lie on the ground, you ARE surrounded, lie on the ground, this is the police."

The Shaman made a spirited dive to the ground, quite agile for his age. Neluka quietly focused on her breath again. Soon the clearing was swarming with policemen and flashlights and Alsatian dogs.

THE LOVERS

CHAPTER 11

THE LOVERS

They didn't want to let each other go, and felt each other's spirits deeply, the oneness of their flesh overriding their personalities. Both wept openly, even Neluka. They didn't know who was older; they didn't care. They were both wearing Menaka's favourite colours, and even Dylan struggled to tell them apart. Rose was sobbing. Ash and Dylan had never seen her in that state before. They were outside Menaka's house. Lionel finally separated them gently.

"Hey, we are all coming to Matara for the New Year holidays, ok? And we must keep the tradition going, you are sisters. And nothing can or should change that."

Manel nodded, too upset to say anything; she was parting with another daughter. She hugged Neluka again, without a word.

"Bye mother, see you in April," Neluka said.

It was Florence's turn next to drown her in her large chest.

"You must Skype us whenever you are free ok? Otherwise you'll hear from me."

They had bought her a spanking new laptop with a pre-paid internet account.

"Bye." Dylan gave her a light kiss on the cheek.

"Thank you for saving me from the tsunami."

"It wasn't me, it was a tough young guy with us, he… he went down. I don't even know his name. I can't even swim," Dylan said.

"Still you tried, thanks, and because of that I found my sister."

"And got kidnapped," Dylan said.

She smiled, full and wide, for the first time. He felt sorry to see her go. Ash gave her a bear hug.

"You are one of us now, see you soon."

Her nature had grown on them.

"Take her safely home Ranjan," Lionel instructed his estate manager, who was behind the wheel. The car was loaded with gifts – Rex and Dorothy had gifted her some expensive jewelry. Meena had sent some of her finest sweet meats with Rose. There was an entire wardrobe of clothes that her adoptive mother had forced on her. They watched as the car disappeared.

"We almost got her killed," Manel said.

"Maannel!" Florence didn't have to say more, and she stopped with a sheepish smile.

"Gosh, it's like a storm's blown over, these past several weeks, I don't want any more excitement," Florence said, releasing a mighty sigh. The crackers went off in a rapid burst; it was noon on New Year's Day.

"Well that bastard deserved what he got, both of them did. And to think it was that woman all along. Unbelievable," Lionel said with a sudden spurt of emotion.

Priyantha had been shot in the leg and was taken to the prison hospital, while Natalie was locked up along with their gang and the exorcist shaman. Priyantha had been infatuated with her, but she was from a social class that was miles above his, and she had used it to exact a heavy price – the crime for her hand.

"She was never going to marry him, but the sucker was too smitten to see it, and you'd think education would kill that sort of crazed superstition. Obviously not," Lionel said with a tired yawn. They had ushered in the New Year at the police station. The sergeant had vanished without a trace.

"And a lesson for all you kids, don't use the Facebook to find romance, you never know what you will get," Manel aunty said.

"No risk of that happening with us is there?" Ash said, winking at

Menaka. She looked away, turning a deep red. While Rose tackled Dylan, he smiled back with a deliciously smitten look.

"I love you, have always loved you," Dylan murmured in Menaka's ear.

He felt her breath nibble on his neck and her hair tickle his cheeks. He could feel her dimpled smile. His heartbeat made him deaf. He already knew her answer.

They were sitting on the rocky seat near Hunas Falls. Menaka was smitten by the location as Dylan had expected, where the water from the falls gently trickled over the dirt track in small rivulets. They were dipping their feet in the refreshingly cold water, and had the place to themselves, except for the goats. Muruga uncle's herd lazed in the pasture across from them, and they laughed as they saw Menaka's old goat strutting about with an imperial air. Beyond the pasture was all forest. They could see the evening mist beginning to challenge in the distance above Horton Plains. He knew it would reach them quickly. Dylan sighed; he wanted to stretch the moment forever.

Menaka suddenly turned her face and planted a kiss on his cheek.

"Why were you so gutless for so long? I was getting sick of waiting."

"I was afraid of losing you. I… I couldn't live with that, that way at least I could be near you and see you."

"What if I fell for someone else, I would have obviously spent more time with him?"

"The thought did occur later," Dylan said. "But then again with me as your sole male bodyguard and Manel aunty's 24-hour surveillance regime, you had no real chance did you?"

"You are an idiot." Menaka craned her head to look at him. He kissed her gently on the lips, soaring with supreme confidence, every nerve ending on his body standing to attention.

"You almost killed me with that Priyantha bullshit, I was mad at him then, I am mad at him now."

"Well, nothing comes cheaply darling, you must earn it. Having said that, you are a bit of a sleaze bag too aren't you?"

"No way, what do you mean?" Dylan was quick with his confident defense.

"Well, you loved me and tried to seduce my sister. How about that?" Menaka broke in to a laugh. Dylan pinched her cheek.

"Dylan?"

"Hmmm?"

"Will... will your parents mind that I am a Buddhist?"

"My God! That's way in the future. And who said we are going to marry anyway?"

Menaka went silent, her eyes misty. Dylan kissed her hair gently.

"I will jump from World's End if I can't get you. I am not letting you go now for anybody, you should know that, feel that. I... I went crazy when you disappeared."

The tears leapt without warning. Menaka straightened up, removed his glasses and kissed them away, one by one.

"I am sorry darling, I am sorry; you'll never lose me, never. You will always be mine."

The ear-splitting shriek froze them – it was right above the falls. Dylan squeezed Menaka against his body. He couldn't move, and they were both trembling. They heard the branches cracking, getting louder, the goats started to bleat and a massive thing jumped right over them. Menaka and Dylan screamed as it grazed their heads, the force rocking them. It landed on the herd with a subhuman and mournful howl. Dylan had his eyes closed, Menaka shook against him. It looked at them, unperturbed, confident of its raw power and its ultimate status on the food chain. It was massively tall with glowing eyes, and had a conspicuous row of small spikes along its back and what looked liked the hind legs of a giant cat. With a final scream, the beast leapt in to the mist and trees, and the old goat vanished with it. There was silence, and Dylan opened his eyes. Menaka was calmly snapping away with his mobile phone camera.

"Wow! That was amazing, did you, did you get it?" he asked excitedly. She returned the camera with a pedestrian yawn.

"It would have been wow if you saw it. You know what? I really might have to hire a real bodyguard after I marry you. You know, just in case," she said with a smile. Dylan looked down.

"And you know something else? I love that too."

"Well, we'll have to find you another old goat," Dylan said with a nervous laugh, still shaken. Menaka laughed.

"I think I have already found one."

"Wow... amazing... you guys had the perfect view... superb... and LOOK at those eyes."

Ash and Rose were talking over each other, fighting for the mobile phone. They were back at the tree house, in broad daylight.

"Hey! Why don't we contact the Geographic guys straight away, why waste time? This is good enough, right?" Ash said.

"What the hell were you doing there anyway? That time of the day, you should have told me, after all I introduced the spot to you." Rose tried to sound offended.

"You know, two's company, three's a crowd," Dylan said sweetly.

"Oh is that so? I will find a nice guy as well and show you, you think I can't?" Rose said, getting rid of the ever-present strand of hair from her face.

"Well, Hamid Khan will get parole in a about a decade's time, you might be in luck then," Dylan said laughing. Rose slapped him hard on the back. Menaka was strangely silent with a faraway look.

"And what's wrong with you now, you want to elope with someone again?" Rose said, waving her hand in front of Menaka's face.

"No, I was just thinking, imagine the fuss if we make these photos public. We might win the million, but... but this place will be flooded with people. They might try to catch it; some might try to kill it. You know some people will always be too greedy."

There was a sudden silence.

"There is a certain... magic, mystery about them, I'd love our children and their own to see it and be awed and inspired, I don't want them to become extinct. What do you think?" Menaka said looking around.

The silence was louder this time. Rose suddenly leaned forward, grabbed the phone and hit the delete button. No one said a word.

"The only thing is, poor Muruga uncle will run out of goats," Rose said with a serious air.

They all laughed, but not as loud as they used to.